Love you

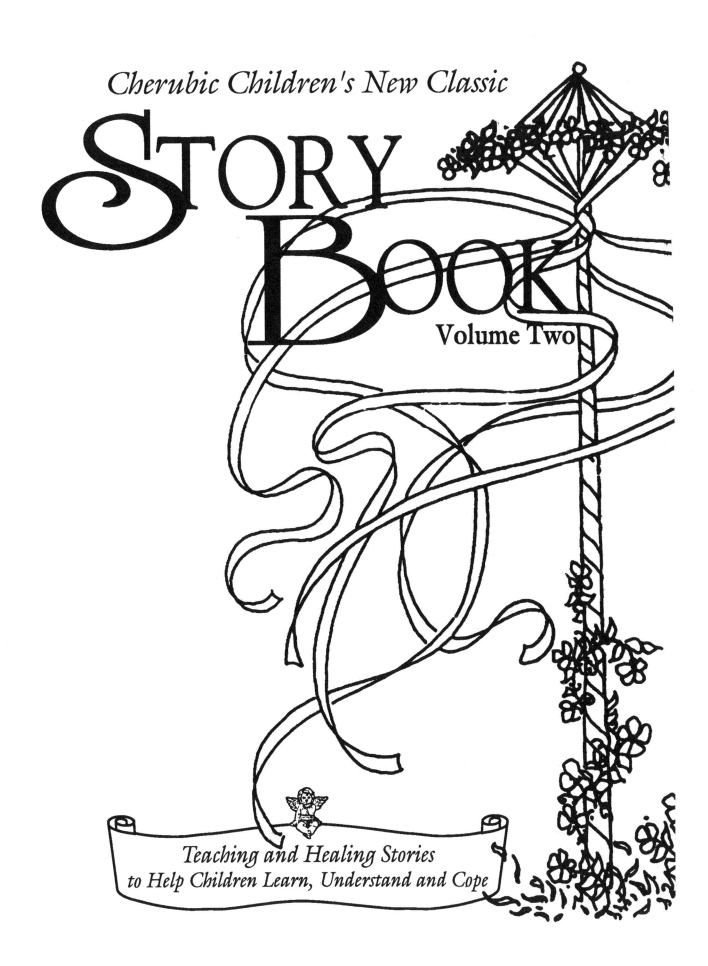

Cherubic Children's New Classic

Story Book

Volume Two

*Teaching and Healing Stories
to Help Children Learn, Understand and Cope*

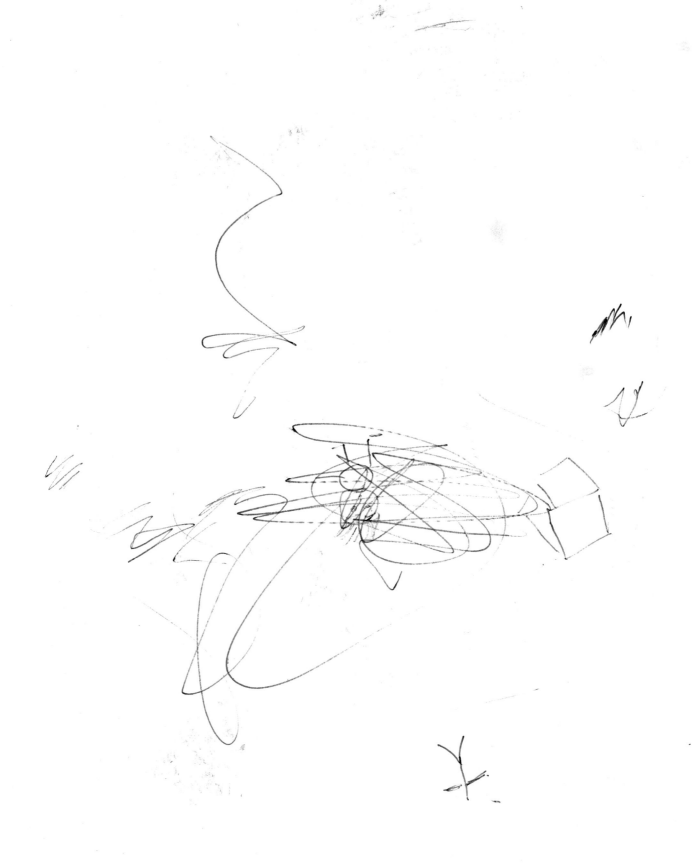

Cherubic Children's New Classic

STORY
BOOK
Volume Two

Teaching and Healing Stories
to Help Children Learn, Understand and Cope

Edited by Juliette Gray

Cherubic Press ~ Johnstown, PA

Published by:

Cherubic Press
P.O. Box 5036
Johnstown, PA 15904

to obtain additional copies of this book send $24.95
plus $5 postage and handling to the above address.

First Printing January 1998

© 1998 Cherubic Press

ISBN 1-889590-24-X

Library of Congress Catalog Card Number: 96-85531

This book features a vinyl laminated cover providing sturdy protection for your child's book while saving natural resources.

Printed in the United States of America

Introduction

by Senior Editor, Juliette Gray

Welcome to *Cherubic Children's New Classic Story Book, Volume Two*. All of us at Cherubic Press are very gratified to know that our first Story Book Collection was so very well received. Now we embark on a second collection, and we have a third and a fourth coming to you as well. For those new to our Story Book collections, you may wonder about our title, "New-Classic." Isn't that a contradiction in terms? We hope so. This collection and this series of collections is of a new genre; not the traditional story book stories at all, but stories we hope will become the "New Classics," replacing some of the rather questionable story book classics with which many of us grew up.

Every story in this book upholds our publishing philosophy to teach or uplift in some way. Each story in this story book is designed to teach children, help them understand and cope with difficult situations, and help them heal and develop into healthy, well-rounded, emotionally stable adults.

It has been a pleasure to work with an extraordinary staff and an honor to work with each and every author and illustrator. I have been very impressed not only with their professionalism but also with their enthusiasm and dedication to help enrich the lives of children.

I would like to thank everyone who helped bring this story book to fruition. I am very fortunate to work in a profession I love and to be able to work with people who have a vision of a better place. A place where children are safe to play, where parents do not have to live in constant fear for their children's emotional, spiritual or physical well-being, and where everyone can come together in a spirit of trust and hope. It was in that spirit that Cherubic Press

Please excuse the poor quality of this photo but it is from Ms. Gray's ID badge, the only photo we could obtain.

developed this book and in that spirit that it now presents this book to you. We hope you agree with us that what has emerged is a book, and a series, that is very special.

CREDITS

Editor in Charge: Juliette Gray

Administration: Julie Dickerson
Diana Herman
SaraBeth Sullivan
Gail Firestone

Submissions Editor: Robert Gratton

Art Coordinator: William Morgan

Art Consultant: Linda Rzoska

Proof Editor: Nicholas Sempeti

Accounting Supervisor: Kevin Dickerson

Legal Consultant: Jay W. Lewis, Esq.

Chapter Markers: Jeannie Hamilton and Juliette Gray

Cover Design: Laura Bryant, Juliette Gray, Julie Dickerson
Kevin Dickerson, William Morgan

Cover Illustration: Laura Bryant

Many thanks to Laura Bryant, illustrator, for the lovely pastel watercolor that graces the cover of this story book. Her delightful rendition of children joyously dancing around a colorful Maypole in a flowered field during Renaissance times, was created especially for this book from design ideas developed by our staff.

We thank Ms. Bryant for her cooperation and professionalism and for a finished product that represents just what we wanted to show; the delights of childhood supported by a circle of concerned adults.

Thank you, Laura.

Table of Contents

The stories are arranged in order within each chapter according to the age level to which they are written.
Stories written for younger children come first in each chapter.

Appreciating Others

Li'l Pop Siggle's Big Surprise

by Denise Irvine Simmons

Dedicated to
Scott, Spencer, and Hunter

Illustrated by Jon Huckeby

Ding! Ding! Ding!

It was a warm day in the last week of summer when the children heard the bells of the ice cream cart coming down the street. They raced from their houses towards the ice cream cart with their money clutched tightly in their hands. Each child was hoping for their favorite flavored ice cream, and each ice cream was hoping for a little boy or girl to love them.

Inside the cart, at the very bottom, the Li'l Pop Siggle was waiting.

The cart was filled with pops of every color and flavor; strawberry, cherry, orange, pineapple, lemon, banana, green apple, blueberry, and purple-grape.

On that warm Monday afternoon, the excited children crowded around the ice cream cart. One little girl, who was much smaller than the others, was pushed to the back of the line. When it was finally her turn, the smallest girl reached into the cart to get her pop, but she didn't find any. It appeared that all of the pops were gone. She walked away slowly with a sad look on her face.

However, although the smallest girl did not see him, Li'l Pop Siggle was in the cart, at the very bottom where no one could see him, waiting and hoping for a little boy or girl to choose him. "Oh, I'm sure a boy or girl will choose me tomorrow!" he said.

On Tuesday, new pops of every color and flavor were placed in the cart on top of Siggle. Throughout the warm day, the other pops dripped and dripped onto him.

Once again, at the end of the day, every pop was chosen except for one: Li'l Pop Siggle.

On Wednesday, Li'l Pop Siggle smiled at the children and hoped that one of them would see him, but no one did. Instead, the other pops kept dripping and dripping onto him, until he was quite a mess!

"I sure hope a boy or girl will choose me tomorrow", he thought nervously. "Summer will be over soon and then the ice cream cart will be put away until next summer. If I am in the cart, I will surely melt! Oh dear!"

On Thursday, the new pops laughed at and teased Li'l Pop Siggle. "What boy or girl would want a pop that looks like THAT?" whispered the red cherry pop to the yellow banana pop.

Siggle was getting worried. "What if the others are right? What if nobody wants me?"

On Friday, the green apple and orange pops laughed at Li'l Pop Siggle.
"We don't like you. You don't look like the rest of us at all!" they said.
The blueberry and grape pops turned away from Siggle and giggled
quietly together.

On Saturday, Li'l Pop Siggle tried and tried to be seen by a boy or girl, but it didn't work. He was lonely and unhappy. "Oh dear," he cried, "no boy or girl will ever want me because I look different. And there is only one more day of summer!"

It was Sunday afternoon, the last day of summer, and once again all of the new pops had been chosen by a boy or girl. But there was one more child still hoping for one. Just then, the last child in line quietly walked up to the cart. It was the smallest girl. With wide eyes, she looked into the cart, but her face slowly saddened as she realized that again, all the pops were gone.

Then she began to cry.

Just then, as she was turning to leave, a smile appeared on the smallest girl's face as she spotted Li'l Pop Siggle at the very bottom of the cart. Siggle looked up at the smallest girl but thought sadly, "I have been dripped and dripped on so much that I am different. She will not want a pop like me."

But to Li'l Pop Siggle's surprise, the smallest girl cheered "Oh, how lucky I am! I will have the most wonderful pop of all!" she said. My pop is *different* from all the others!"

She reached down into the cart and proudly lifted Siggle high into the air for everyone to see. Li'l Pop Siggle was *beautiful!*

"My pop is every color of the rainbow: red, orange, yellow, green, blue, and purple!" she laughed. "And it isn't just one flavor. It has the flavors of all the other pops - - strawberry, cherry, orange, pineapple, lemon, banana, green apple, blueberry, and purple-grape!"

When the other children saw how wonderful the smallest girl's pop was, they wanted one, too. However, they soon learned that Siggle was special. There was only one like him.

Li'l Pop Siggle was as happy as he could be. As the smallest girl smiled and held him tightly, Li'l Siggle shouted proudly "I *like* being different!"

Denise Irvine Simmons

is a wife and mother residing in Orange County, California, with her husband, Scott, and their two young sons, Spencer and Hunter. In 1989, following the completion of her bachelor's degree in Legal Studies and English Ms. Simmons began her professional writing career. Until recently, it consisted primarily of legal research, writing, and teaching. Inspired by the stories she was reading to her children, Ms. Simmons decided to diverge from her legal/technical writing background and devote her writing talents to projects which she considered much more rewarding: creative writing for children This story, Ms. Simmons' first effort, is based upon a family bedtime story told to her by her mother, which she remembers from early childhood. Currently, Ms. Simmons is working on her next children's book. She wishes to extend special thanks to her father for all of his encouragement and support.

Jon Huckeby

says that he was two years old when he first picked up a pencil and every day since then he has drawn something. He said 'I even draw in my sleep". This is the first children's story he has illustrated. Mr. Huckeby spends most of his time illustrating for Tomato Cards in Kansas City, Missouri, where he lives with his wife, Paula.

We Can All Play

by Nasreen Razack

*Dedicated to My Dear Father,
Dr. Mohamed S. Razack*

Illustrated by Earl L. Martin, III

Children the world over, listen to me.
There is something important to hear and to see.
I want you to know that we can all play;
I want you to know we can start today.

Whether you're yellow, white, black, brown, or red,
No matter what anyone has said,

I want you to know that we can all play;
I want you to know that we can start today.

Hey, Mr. Bird up in the tree,
Take a really good look at me.
Do I look different with a different sounding name?

That's OK because inside we are all the same.
Human beings, that's what we are.
That's what you'll find if you travel near or far.

25

Listen to me, please, my school teacher;
Listen to me, please, my religious preacher;

I have a message I'm sending loud and clear:
Being different is nothing to fear!

27

I have a dream that one day we will be
Eating ice cream, singing happily,

All holding hands, all nations together,
All being friends forever and ever.

I can play with all of you,
Whether you are brown, red, yellow or blue!
Oh! What a shame and what a disgrace
To not play with someone because of their race!

Remember no matter what anyone may say
I want you to know that we can all play.
Just as oysters contain beautiful pearls
We are all beautiful boys and girls.
No two alike, yet we're sister and brother.
Never forget, we can play with each other!

Nasreen Razack

was born on March 15, 1971 in Rochester, New York. She is a first generation American of Indian/Pakistani origin. Ms. Razack is currently a third year medical student at St. George's University School of Medicine. The author states "I have felt it is important to break cultural and racial barriers at a young age. After all, we all come from one common origin." Ms. Razack currently lives in Williamsville, New York.

Earl L. Martin, III

born in Atlanta, Georgia, Earl grew up in Montgomery, Alabama where he graduated from the Montgomery Academy. He attended the University of Virginia as an Echols scholar where he graduated in 1996 with majors in math and cognitive science. Earl has been sketching since he was a very young boy. He has taken art classes and has pursued computerized animation as well as free-hand drawing on his own time. His other interests include reading fiction, juggling, puzzles, computer programming, and old movies. In the fall of 1996 he began law school at Emory Law School on full scholarship. That year he also illustrated a story in Cherubic Children's New Classic Story Book, Volume One, which was written by his sister.

THE MOUSE HOUSE

by Audrey Spilker

Dedicated to
Erica Robin Sunkin

illustrated by Miriam Sagasti

Once upon a time in a beautiful kingdom, there was a magical palace.

It was filled with lots of secret hiding places where one could always make
new friends and enjoy all sorts of adventures.

One particularly exciting spot to play in the palace was located in a corner of the hall closet. That's where one could find the Mouse House.

Inside the Mouse House lived the Mouse family. The family was made up of Mommy Mouse, Daddy Mouse, and Baby Mouse.

Sometimes, Daddy Mouse or Mommy Mouse would have to leave the Mouse House to find food for the family. After all, they were the breadwinners, and they would take turns going on business trips to the palace kitchen.

If it was an especially long trip, Mommy Mouse or Daddy Mouse would spend the night at the Roach Motel which was run by Mrs. Roach and all of her four-hundred children. The Roach's Motel was another magical place in the palace and could only be found hidden away, under the kitchen sink.

Sometimes, if Baby Mouse was behaving especially well, Mommy Mouse and Daddy Mouse would surprise her with a little vacation. Mice, as I'm sure you know, are excellent travelers and enjoy new experiences.

Baby Mouse's favorite place to journey to was the country, which existed in the rose bushes outside in the palace garden. That's where Captain Cricket and his band "The String Crickette" would play their instruments all night long; sometimes accompanied by Sergeant Spider on the web.

Baby Mouse would sing and dance along to the music until it was time to return to the Mouse House to go to bed.

One day, a condominium went up next door to the Mouse House and caused
quite a commotion among the palace residents. Everybody in the kingdom
showed up at the Mouse House for a neighborhood meeting. Mommy Mouse
made her famous cheesecake and B. Bumble brought his award winning
honey pie. Everyone was in high spirits, although they had come for a serious
discussion.

The meeting came to order when Nat Gnat flew to the top of the Mouse
House ceiling and announced in a loud voice, "The neighborhood is in grave
danger!" This silenced most of the buzzing that was going about. Nat Gnat
continued, "When a condominium goes up in a neighborhood, that means
only one thing - - Felines!"

Everybody was quiet with fear.

Now, nobody in the kingdom had ever seen a feline, much less spoken to one, but they were sure they didn't like them. So when Nat Gnat called for the Possum Posse to take action against the new neighbors, his words were met with thunderous wing clapping and paw stomping.

With that, the meeting was adjourned and everybody went home to their respective houses, nests and hives throughout the palace grounds.

The next day, all the palace residents, protected by the Possum Posse and the Insect Infantry, marched their way to the despised condominium, stopping, at last, by the Mouse House to pick up the Mouse family.

As the gang approached the house, they heard a high pitched squeak and out of the Mouse House ran Mommy and Daddy Mouse. "We can't find Baby Mouse anywhere!" shrieked Mommy Mouse to all those who had gathered.

"Maybe the felines got hold of her!" exclaimed Daddy Mouse.

"Don't you worry my dears!" shouted Sergeant Spider, "We'll get your kid back from the wretched felines!"

"Yes, yes," chimed in Captain Cricket. "I was specially trained in the military for these types of situations, although I have been a civilian all these years, I've still got what it takes!"

Now at this point, everyone was riled up and more high strung than usual. It took them awhile to settle down and focus on the fact that while they were planning and plotting their attacks and ambushes, a big fluffy creature had emerged from the condominium, followed by a smaller fluffy creature, who was then followed by Baby Mouse who appeared to be perfectly healthy.

Apparently, to the astonishment of all who gathered, Baby Mouse had been playing checkers all morning long at the home of her new best friend, Kit, who had moved next door with her mother, Mrs. Cats.

Of course Mrs. Cats was surprised to see the huge crowd around her condominium and asked if everything was all right.

At that moment, Nat Gnat fluttered to the front of the group and said, "Why yes, dear Madam, everything is perfectly fine. We all wanted to welcome personally yourself and your precious child to our humble neighborhood."

"Yippee, Hooray!" cried everybody.

Mommy Mouse and Daddy Mouse said that since they lived so close, all were invited to the Mouse House for a celebration in honor of their new found friends and neighbors. Of course they all went and had a wonderful time.

It certainly was a magical palace.

Audrey Spilker

is a twenty-three year old native of Los Angeles, California and a recent graduate of Loyola Marymount University, where she received her degree in Theater Arts. She plans on continuing writing for children as well as pursuing a career in playwriting and other areas of fiction. She was inspired to create *The Mouse House* by her five year old cousin, Erica. Audrey would like to thank her family and friends for their loving and unwavering support for all of her creative endeavors.

Ms. Sagasti and her dog, Pretzel

Miriam Sagasti

was born in Lima, Peru. She attended the School of Interior Design in Lima, Peru and the National Agrarian University where she studied landscaping, also in Lima, Peru. After she came to the United States in 1978, she studied graphic design, illustration and photography at N.V.C.C. in Virginia. From 1983 to 1990 she received awards and recognition in over twenty art shows, exhibitions, and competitions across the United States and in Peru. Her work was also selected to the 1994 International Children's Books Illustration Fair in Bologna, Italy, was selected for the Best of International Self Promotion Books by the Supon Design Group, and for the Letterhead and Logo Design 3 held by Rockport Publishers. Ms. Sagasti says she always wanted to do illustrations for children's literature and about five years ago began sending out samples of her art to children's book publishers. Since that time Ms. Sagasti's work has been published in seven of the Barron's Educational Series books on occupations, in three of Kar-Ben Copies books about the Jewish tradition, in two books by the Mennonite Press, and two by Concordia Publishing House. She has illustrated several articles in *Teaching K-8 Magazine,* and has illustrated several articles and done covers for *Hopscotch Magazine for Girls* and *Boy's Quest Magazine.* She has also illustrated seven puzzles for The Great American Puzzle Factory and has illustrated a book for Quarasan's Project Take Home Books. Ms. Sagasti has three children who are all in graduate school at the present time. She and her husband, Leo, an architect, have recently moved from Herndon, Virginia to their current residence in Chapel Hill, North Carolina.

A Special Story

by Marion Kozlowski

Dedicated to Dr. Phillip Decker
who has been my inspirational force in story writing,
and to all the children of the world who, for the first time,
will walk the unknown path that will lead them into a world of caring, understanding,
and above all, love, for their new found friends.

Illustrated by Jenna Rogers

Many weeks had past since kindergartners in Miss James' class first started school. They all seemed very happy going to school and being with their new friends. All the children seemed to get along well with one another. Everyone knew each others name and they all had learned the first lesson in sharing. They learned to pay attention and listen when Miss James spoke. The children always looked forward to the time when Miss James had them form their circle on the floor. This was their signal that story time was about to start.

On this particular day, Miss James chose to read a "special story" about a very special little boy. This story would prepare the children for another lesson in life. The story was titled "Not Like Me".

The children looked at each other wondering what would be so different about the special little boy in the story.

As Miss James read the story, the children thought the little boy was just like them until she came to the part that spoke of his having only partial fingers. All the children looked at their own fingers and couldn't imagine not having long, whole fingers.

This was exactly what Miss James was expecting them to do.

Miss James rose from her seat and showed each child, on their very own hand, what it would be like not to have long, whole fingers. Knowing the children understood, she continued the story.

She told how the little baby was born with what the doctors called a "birth imperfection".

As the baby grew, his mother felt bad. She was afraid that when it came time for her little boy to go to school, the other children would laugh and make fun of him.

This thought made the little boy's mommy very sad. Miss James showed the picture of the little boy in the story to the children. Except for shorter fingers, the children thought the little boy looked just like them.

When Miss James finished the story, one of the children asked if it was really a true story. The answer to the question was "yes" and that question was followed by many more.

The children wanted to know the answers. This was Miss James' purpose in telling them the story. Miss James was amazed at the questions and input from the small children.

Miss James answered their questions in a way that helped the children really understand. They spoke about the baby's birth and how sad it was for the mommy and daddy. How the parents worried about how the other children would laugh and make fun of their little boy.

It was then that Miss James explained how easy it is to be born with a "birth imperfection" and how lucky every one was who was not born with an "imperfection". The children looked at their fingers and at each other and truly realized how lucky they were.

Miss James spoke of other imperfections such as blindness, deafness, loss of arms or legs and diseases that put children in wheelchairs.

Miss James said, "Close your eyes and imagine your body being a car. It gets you around and it takes you where you want to go. Some cars are big, some small, some old, some new. But remember; it's not the body of the car that matters, it's what's inside the car. Remember, understanding, caring, love and kindness all come from within ourselves."

We shine from within and when we shine bright enough, it shows through to our outer shell.

A beautiful smile is a great example.

It doesn't matter how many fingers, arms or legs you have. It doesn't matter if you have a "birth imperfection". Remember, it doesn't change who you really are. You still feel love and warmth; you still cry and laugh and you still feel pain, hurt and disappointment.

We can all relate to these things, so you see, we really aren't any different except for having a more perfect outer body. The purpose of this special story is when you meet a special girl or boy - - TALK! Make them a friend.

Your warmth and friendliness will make their fears go away and you will be a true winner because you just made a shining, new friend.

Then Miss James told them some news! Soon a little boy who had been born with an "imperfection" would be in their very own class!

The children in Miss James class could hardly wait to share their story at home and were all looking ahead to meeting their new, very special friend.

Marion Kozlowski

who describes herself as a "spiritually motivated writer of inspirational children's stories", says the reason that she, a sixty-one-year-young grandmother of ten grandchildren, decided to start on the new adventure of story writing at this point in her life, is because of the requests of her own grandchildren to read them a story. She wants "to put on paper the lessons in our every-day living that affects all of us from the earliest age to those of us over sixty, who realize that we are never too old to learn, even if it's from children's books." She says she wants to write stories that are beneficial in helping small children who are just starting on the road to life's adventure. As the

author says, "Let's help to keep the young minds and hearts open and on the right path to making our world a more caring, friendlier, and happier place." Ms. Kozlowski lives in Michigan, enjoys travel, and has written several other children's stories. She says that she is "encouraged and uplifted on my spiritual voyage of spiritual practicality by my husband, Edward, our four children, ten loving grandchildren, and two chihuahua pups, Honey and Sugar."

Jenna Rogers

was born and raised in Kentucky. With her illustrations in this book, she makes her professional debut as an illustrator. Ms. Rogers studied art at ACA College of Design in Cincinnati, Ohio, and plans on furthering her career as an illustrator. She currently lives in Hebron, Kentucky, with her husband.

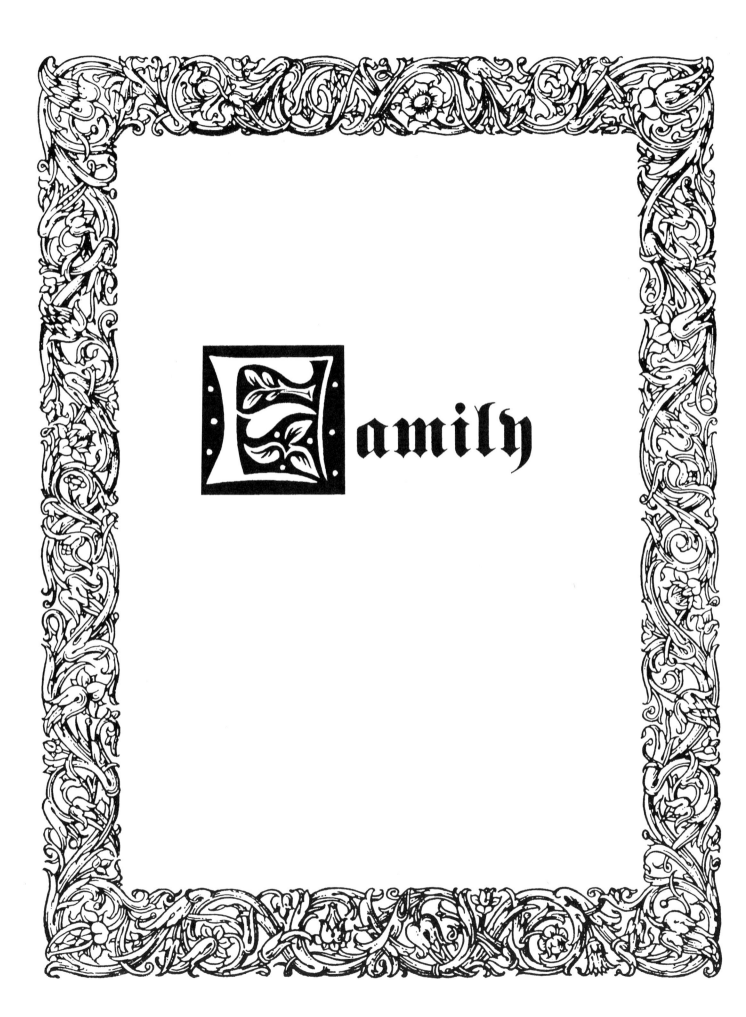

Family

Helen Grace and Her New Book

by **Maria Picciano**

Dedicated to
My Daughter

Illustrated by Margaret Picciano

Sit down here Grandma and read to me.
Too soon for my nap and snack's not till three.

This book is special - - only pictures, no words.

Everything in it's familiar, including the birds.

Look at this hat, we have one like that.

I bet it fits you, it fits me, how about that!

And what about this, it's a flower, a rose.
Here's one for you and one for my nose.

Look at these toys, I've seen them before.
Oh yes they're like mine, right here on the floor.

This house looks like ours, painted yellow and green,
with a beautiful garden, the best I have seen.

Oh, here's Daddy's picture.
I look just like him,
but also like Mommy,
the same hair and chin.

And who's this girl Grandma?
This looks like my face.

I know who it is, it's me, Helen Grace!

Maria Picciano

was born December 2, 1964 in the Bronx, NY. She graduated from Johnson and Whales University in Providence, RI, with an associates degree in business in 1985. In high school she rewrote "The Odyssey" for use as a text to help students better understand the book. She excelled in English Literature in high school and won state and local poetry contests during those years. In college she tutored English as a second language to foreign students. Currently she works as a bookkeeper and she and her husband take care of their young daughter.

Margaret Picciano

was born February 20, 1961, in the Bronx, NY. Although she says she has been drawing "since I could hold a pencil," her formal art training was at State University of New York in Buffalo, NY, 1979-1980. She graduated from SUNY, Stonybrook, NY, with a degree in biology. She won numerous awards in grammar school including the best dental display in sixth grade and the best Christmas display in fifth grade. When she was in the eighth grade, she constructed and painted a mural on the basement walls of Sagamore Junior High School. She says she draws "as a pastime" and has "always enjoyed drawing cartoons and caricatures, oils for portraits and inks for cartoons." Ms. Picciano is also a licensed practical nurse and is currently working in a dialysis clinic in Hempstead, New York.

Leaving the Nest

by Janice Saber Michael

Dedicated to my parents, Stephen and Betty,
for showing me how to enjoy life.
My husband, Van, who always gives me love and support in all I do.
My children, Kevin and Kaylene, who are my inspiration to write,
and the pair of robins who build their nest every spring on our front porch.

Illustrated by Margie Moore

Kaylene was seven years old.

She lived with her mom, dad and brother in a pink brick house. In her front yard was a large crab-apple tree which had many fluffy blossoms in the spring.

67

Kaylene's brother was much older than she was. His name was Kevin. He was going to college in the fall. He had decided that it was time for him to move out of their house and get his own apartment.

Kaylene didn't understand why Kevin would want to move out of their home. She was very sad.

One day Kaylene was sitting at the kitchen table coloring. Her mom was at the counter packing some dishes in a box for Kevin to take to his apartment. Kaylene noticed that her mom looked sad too.

Kaylene asked her, "Mommy, are you sad?"

"Well, yes. I guess I am," her mom replied.

"Why?" Kaylene asked.

"I am sad because Kevin is leaving the nest," she answered.

"What?" Kaylene laughed. "We don't live in a nest!"

Her mother giggled, "It's just an expression. Let me explain to you what it means."

Kaylene followed her mom over to the couch. They sat down. Her mom put her arm around Kaylene and pointed out the front window to a robin's nest. Every spring a pair of robins built a nest in the big crab-apple tree.

Kaylene's mom began to explain. "Do you remember what happened last year after the baby robins hatched from their eggs?" she asked.

"I think so. The mom and dad robins fed the baby robins and they grew bigger every day," Kaylene said.

"That's right," her mother replied. "But do you remember what happened after that?"

Kaylene looked puzzled. "I think I forgot," she answered.

"Well," her mom continued. "They did grow bigger and bigger every day. In fact, they began to look bigger than their parents because their feathers were so fluffy."

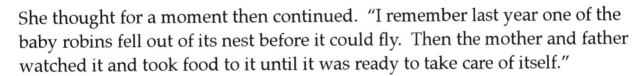

She thought for a moment then continued. "I remember last year one of the baby robins fell out of its nest before it could fly. Then the mother and father watched it and took food to it until it was ready to take care of itself."

"Then the time came when they were ready to leave their nest. They didn't all leave on the same day though. The first one to leave was probably the biggest or strongest or maybe the most adventureous. Each one stood on the edge of the nest and flapped their wings to see if they were strong enough to fly," mother recalled.

"Then at last there was one baby robin left in the nest. Maybe the last baby to leave was the smallest, the weakest or just liked the security of the nest," Mom explained.

Kaylene giggled, "I think the baby stayed in the nest because it wanted the whole nest to itself."

"This is probably true," mother laughed.

"Anyway, that is what I meant when I said that Kevin was leaving the nest," she continued. "He is leaving the home where he grew up and venturing out to live on his own just like the baby robins. If he is not ready, like the baby who fell out, your dad and I will help him. It is a normal part of growing up. It is good to become independent."

"What does independent mean?" Kaylene questioned.

"It means not depending on others but learning to depend on yourself," mother answered.

Kaylene looked puzzled, "If it is good for Kevin to be independent and it is good for Kevin to move away then why do you feel sad?"

"Well now," her mom replied, "I am sad for the same reason that you are sad. We are used to seeing Kevin every day and we are going to miss him very much."

Kaylene looked sad, "I will miss saying good-night to him every night," she said.

Mother took Kaylene's hand as she explained. "See, in life sometimes events that are good can also make us feel sad. Sometimes we just have to get used to the change. Just think about how much fun it will be for us to call Kevin on the phone or go to visit him in his apartment. You'll see. It will be okay."

Kaylene was quiet. "What's wrong?" her mother questioned.

Kaylene asked, "Is it okay if I stay in the nest for a long, long time?"

Mother smiled, "That sounds like a great idea," she said, and gave Kaylene a big hug.

Janice Saber Michael

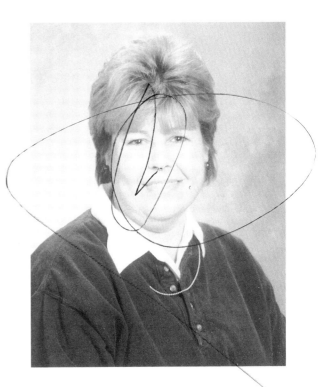

was born and raised near Pittsburgh, PA. She met her husband in high school and was married a year after graduation. They have been married for 23 years and have a son, Kevin, who is 21 years old, and a daughter, Kaylene, who is 13. Ms. Michael says she decided to go to college when she was 38. She attended Lorain County Community College where she received an associate degree in psychology. "While attending college," the author says, "I realized I wanted to work in the area of child psychology. But, I have always had a desire to write as well." Ms. Michael combined those areas with the writing of this story. As she says, "I believe that through writing children's books, I can reach many children and help them with their problems and concerns." She says she wrote *Leaving the Nest*, not only because it is about an issue her family dealt with personally, but also "because in today's world children experience change more frequently than past generations. Relocations due to divorce and job transfers are very common. I believe that, as parents, we need to make our children realize that change is a necessary part of life and teach them to remain optimistic as they deal with their feelings about their future."

Margie Moore

first fell in love with children's illustration as a child growing up in Belmar, a New Jersey shore town. She frequently visited the library to take out her favorite books. In early adulthood she began to draw and to study the work of early 20th century artists famous for children's illustration, especially those who did fantasy work. She herself works mostly in a whimsical style in pen & ink and watercolor. She hopes that one day her illustrations will become endearing like the ones that inspired her as a child. Margie now lives in West Belmar, New Jersey with her husband and three daughters who look very much like the little girl in this story.

The Sleepyland Slide

by David H. Lasaine

*Dedicated to My Buddies,
Shelby and Kelly;
you'll always be in my heart.*

Illustrated by Guy Smalley

A tiny voice cried out in the middle of the night. "Whaaat?" asked a deep voice from another room.

"I had a bad dream," answered the little voice.

Into the room walked the creature that played games, tickled without mercy, made giant hot-fudge sundaes, told the best bedtime stories, and could turn tears into smiles.

75

"Daddy, would you tell me a story?"

Before Dad could answer, the bunk above Kelly began to shake. Out from a pile of fluffy blankets popped the head of his brother, Shelby.

"Tell me too!" he asked.

"You guys are really something," Dad said while reaching to turn on the lamp. He sat down in the story chair. This was no ordinary chair. It was covered with soft, deep red, velvet cloth. The back was spread like a peacock's tail and had arms as thick as tree trunks. On the bottom of this huge chair were four tiny wooden legs with birds feet.

Dad took a deep breath and let it out slowly, turning his neck and stretching his arms to get rid of stiffness.

"Hurry up!" Kelly insisted.

Dad turned, gave him a stern look then cleared his throat, "Ahem!" Then he smiled, "Here we go guys . . . to a land far away."

"It's a land of sweet things.

A place to play.

Where you can laugh and giggle for all the day.

So - -

Hold on tight,

We're going on a journey

that could last all night!"

"Many miles away is a beautiful place where you can see, touch, hear, and taste the things which are only in your dreams. The trees and plants are very colorful. The water is so clear you can see the fish swimming lazily about. There are strange looking animals not seen in the zoo that will ask you to play with them. And in this land is a magical slide! The glitter in it sparkles in the sunlight. The steps are giant and colorful. It twists and turns way up, up into the sky. This is the Sleepland Slide!"

Shelby held his Mr. Monkey tightly to his chest, and Kelly held his Applesauce the Rabbit. Their minds began to see the slide. Suddenly a huge, smooth bright green step appeared.

"This slide is so high!" said Kelly as he tilted his head back.

"And it doesn't end!" exclaimed Shelby.

As the boys climbed on the first step, it flashed to fantastic orange!

"Wow!" shouted Kelly.

"Watch me!" yelled Shelby, as he leapt from spot to spot to change the colors from pink, to yellow, to purple.

Dad shouted, "Look at the sides and you'll see shapes and letters from every language too."

After climbing awhile, they were surrounded by puffy, white clouds. The boys stretched for a piece of the cloud to taste. They looked at each other and laughed.

"It tastes like candy," said Shelby.

Dad reached for a piece. WHOOSH! Green and red feathers filled the air.

"That was close!" exclaimed Dad, pulling feathers from his hair.

"What was that?" laughed Kelly.

"Gizeeble-gizable," said Dad. "He will swoop down on you and stick his long, skinny, ice cream cone-shaped beak in your ear and laugh while tickling you with his big yellow feet. They are quite silly creatures."

"Let's go higher!" shouted Shelby.

The climb continued. Before they knew it, they were right next to the moon.
The boys looked at their Dad. He knew what they wanted. He nodded his
head and off the slide they went. When they landed on the moon's surface
they bounced around like ping pong balls.

Shelby and Kelly looked at each other as the ground began to shake. From the ground rose a gigantic, crater-covered, smiling, Mr. Man in the Moon.

"Hello, boys. I see you're climbing the slide. Would you like some green cheese? This has been quite a busy season for climbers. Just two weeks ago, a little girl brought along her dog. What a good time we had! I'm still finding bones the dog buried in me. OHHHHH," he moaned.

Mr. Moon looked at the slide. "Why, I'll be a cheese ball! Is that who I think it is? Come on down young man! I haven't seen you since I was. . ."

"That's right," shouted Dad, "not since the last time you were blue, Mr. Moon!" Then he jumped high in the air, did a double somersault and landed next to the boys. "These are my sons. I'm taking them on the Sleepyland Slide tonight."

After playing and running for what seemed like hours, the boys wanted to go home to bed. Kelly pulled on his dad's pants leg and said, "I'm tired, Daddy."

"Yes," answered a tired father. "So am I." Dad climbed back onto the slide and caught his boys in his strong arms.

"GOODNIGHT, MR. MOON!" they shouted.

"Goodnight!" Mr. Moon called back.

81

The top of the slide was now close and the boys said they were scared. Dad hugged them and said, "When I was a little boy I was scared too. I didn't know what was ahead, but just as my father was with me, I will be with you."

Filled with confidence, the boys continued and after a few minutes, reached the top of the slide.

Before them was a view so pretty. The sun's rays bounced off the sugar crystals within the clouds. The mountains below were large scoops of yellow ice-cream covered with rainbow sparkles. A river of dark brown hot fudge had ships of marshmallows floating around islands of whip cream. The trees in the forest were tall thick lollipops. The roads were built of red, blue, green, orange, and pink jelly beans. A volcano was spewing caramel taffy high into the air. Across the deep, green landscape, a herd of twistyneckspringswallows bounced.

This was SLEEPYLAND!

"Are you ready for the ride down?" asked Dad.

"YES!" screamed the boys.

"Then let's GOOOOOoooooooo. . . "

Down they went, tumbling and
turning and laughing, round and
round the Sleepyland Slide.

On the way they saw
chocolate horses eating candy hay!

By the way,
did you ever hear a cow Meow?

Or see a chicken pickin'
cherries for a pie?

How 'bout a jackal,
cackle?

A Fregmellian Frog
wildly dancing on a log?

Well, they did.

On their flight,

This magical night,

Down the Sleepyland Slide.

The next moment the boys were in their beds. Shelby giggled, "Goodnight Dad," as he gave his father a monster hug.

Kelly, whose eyes were now closed, touched his father's face with his little hand. He smiled. "Dad?" he asked.

"Yes?"

"Why is your skin so rough?"

"THAT my son, is another story."

The next morning was bright and cheery. The boys found Dad in the bathroom shaving.

"Dad, guess what?" The boys began talking about a trip with a magical slide, a talking moon, candied clouds, a tickling bird. Their mouths couldn't keep up with their minds.

"Sure, guys. There's probably a Gizeeble-gizable in the kitchen. Please get dressed and straighten your rooms. It'll be a blue moon before you get them clean. It was all just a dream."

They started to walk away, then stopped, and looked at each other. "GIZEEBLE-GIZABLE?   DAAADDD!"

Dad hadn't noticed the tiny red feather in his hair.

David Lasaine

was born in Baltimore, MD, but has lived in the Chicago area most of his life and completed his schooling there. After a failed marriage, he took on the responsibility of raising his two sons, Shelby and Kelly from the time they were toddlers. He continues to find ways to keep his family together, he says, "against all odds in a society in which the mother is usually left to fight the battle." Story-telling is one avenue Mr. Lasaine has found useful in bringing a smile to the faces

Mr. Lasaine with his sons, Shelby and Kelly

of his children. His hobbies include collecting interesting, old books, coins, photography, coaching his sons' baseball team, and, of course, his children. Mr. Lasaine says he has told bedtime stories to his sons "from the day they were born," and decided to write this one down, challenging himself to build on the content of this special story. It originated on a stormy night three years ago, when he and his sons were living in a shelter in Chicago. His younger son, Kelly woke up crying, and Mr. Lasaine went to him and began making up this story, The Sleepyland Slide. He says he hopes this story "will bring smiles to your children's faces as it has to the many children I have read it to so far." Mr. Lasaine hopes that the publishing of this story will raise some funds towards the education of his sons. He says, "Shelby loves the arts and Kelly loves sports." Toward this end, Mr. Lasaine is offering a limited number of signed, hand made, soft pillows for purchase for that special little child to hold during storytime. For more information about the pillows contact Cherubic Press.

Guy Smalley

attended the School of Visual Arts and has won numerous awards, including the Best of Gannett for Graphic Design. He worked as a Graphic Designer for Gannett Corporation for seven years. He also worked as Air Director at Holt, Rinehart & Winston, and at Harcourt Brace Jonovich. He was president of his own advertising agency, SmallKaps Association, for fourteen years, working on such major accounts as Wendy's and McDonalds Ronald McDonald House. He currently owns and operates Mountain Creek Bed & Breakfast Inn in Waynesville, North Carolina, while he continues to illustrate children's books, greeting cards, and various graphic design projects.

There's Always Tomorrow

by Linda Valentino

Dedicated to Dan Visceglie.
Also to his family, who have made it possible for Dan
to see the world through their eyes.

Illustrated by Ned Butterfield

When I was born, my mom and dad named me Daniel - - after my Grandpa
Daniel. Grandpa moved in with us two years ago. I had to share a room with
my older brother Ted, so Grandpa could sleep in my room. I wasn't too
happy about it at first. But Grandpa told me his room would always be my
room too, and I could come in any time.

Every night I brought one of my favorite books into Grandpa's room. He read every word, even on the long pages. We laughed together at some of the pictures. Sometimes he read in a silly voice, and we laughed some more.

Grandpa and I took long walks together. He said we were going to
walk all the way to China. He showed me everything. Grandpa
pointed to the squirrels climbing up and down the nut trees in our backyard.
He always found deer tracks in the snow. In springtime,
we would go looking for birds building nests and babies being fed by mother
robins. We never quite made it to China. I usually got tired of walking.
Grandpa would say, "There's always tomorrow," and we
would head for home.

Grandpa and I did lots of things together. Then our walks started
getting shorter. Grandpa didn't see the nests in the trees or the baby
 birds eating worms.

At story time, he didn't read all the words or laugh at the pictures.

Dad told me Grandpa was going blind. The words in my books looked blurry to Grandpa and got harder to see every day. He no longer could see the animals in the woods. They were beginning to only look like shadows. Dad said even though Grandpa couldn't see well, we could still share our special times together.

Each night I still go into Grandpa's room with one of my favorite books. Now that I'm learning to read, I read to Grandpa. When I get stuck, I spell the word and Grandpa helps me out. I tell him about the funny pictures and we laugh. Then I read in a silly voice and we laugh some more.

Now I take Grandpa on walks. He holds my arm, and I tell him we are
going to walk all the way to China. I tell Grandpa about all the animals I
see and how nice the flowers look. We never quite make it to China.

Grandpa usually gets tired.

I say to Grandpa, "There's always tomorrow," and we head for home.

Linda Valentino

was born in New Jersey and grew up in New York. She graduated from the State University of New York at Cortland with a bachelor of arts in elementary education and art. The author received a master's degree from the State University of New York at New Paltz in elementary education. Ms. Valentino has taught elementary school and art at the Minisink Valley School District in Slate Hill, NY, for twenty years. She resides with her husband, Bill, and two children, Jamie and Craig, in Slate Hill, New York.

Ned Butterfield

is an illustrator of many years experience who lives and works in Islip, New York.

Grandma's Miracles

by Diane-Ellen McCarron

*Dedicated to the Memory of My Grandmother,
Mary Anacka Karaban,
and to all grandmothers everywhere.*

Illustrated by Marilyn Lucey

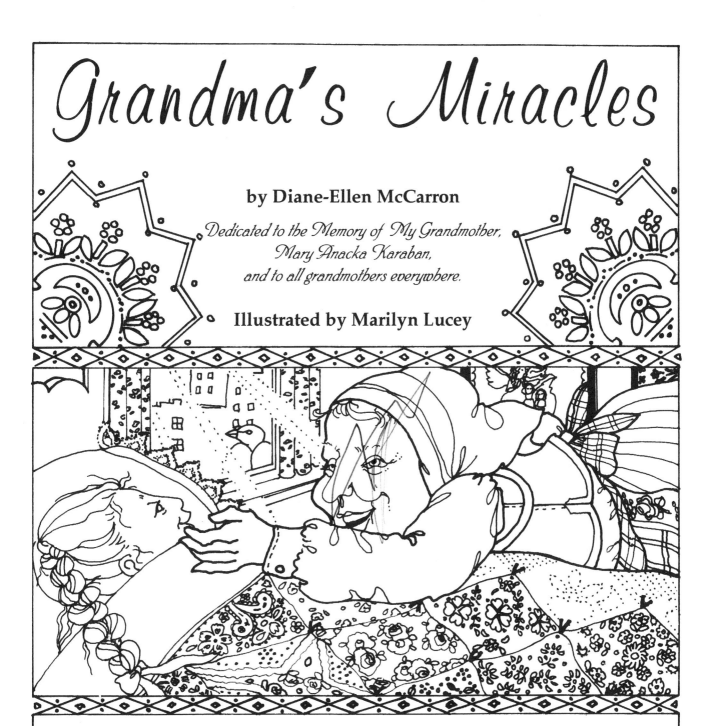

Grandma would wake me up in the unheated room where I slept, covered tightly with a hand-sewn patchwork quilt made from old cloth scraps. Grandma's smile would be sunshine warming the musty room and her eyes would announce the beginning of a special day. Everyday was special to Grandma, because Grandma believed in miracles.

I would sit up in bed, and point to the hand-sewn quilt. Each scrap represented a family milestone and had its home in Grandma's heart. Grandma loved giving the stories in her heart to me.

As Grandma poured pancake batter on the griddle on the iron stove, she would sing soft melodies in words that were unfamiliar to me. Her long patchwork skirt which touched the top of her laced shoes would swish around as she moved.

Grandma would hurry me over to watch the first bubble appear in the cooking batter and we would count each new bubble as a miracle as it popped up. Then Grandma's skirt would swish again as she took her turn flipping one of the pancakes.

We would cook pancakes and more pancakes and then more. She would bring them smothered in butter and syrup to the table and I would eat until I had to unfasten the waistband on my skirt to make room for more.

Grandma would look at me lovingly, and convince me that growing children must eat well in order to be healthy.

After breakfast, Grandma would spread a checked cloth on the table. She would speak of the miracle of gratitude as she tenderly placed a slab of kielbasa, some dark bread, a bunch of cherries, a chunk of cheese, and a quart of milk on top of the cloth. Then she would carefully wrap the food in it. She would put a pad of paper and a pencil into a wicker basket and place the checked bundle on top.

Grandma would cover her shoulders with a woven shawl and cover her head with a babushka that tied under her chin. She would open her bureau drawer and take out another babushka and woven shawl which was wrapped neatly in newspaper and waiting just for me. The babushka and woven shawl had belonged to her small daughter who died from pneumonia many years ago.

Then Grandma and I would climb down five flights of stairs to the ground floor. Grandma wearing her high laced shoes, her long patchwork skirt, her woven shawl and her babushka, and I proudly wearing my babushka and woven shawl with my pink blouse and gray pleated skirt.

Grandma's one hand would clutch the handle of her wicker basket, and her other hand would hold mine. We would be off for an outing for the day. We would stop behind her apartment building to check her vegetable patch. We would look for little changes in the seedlings. Sometimes, a green tomato from the day before turned red. At another time, we would discover a cucumber ready to be picked hiding beneath the vines. There were always lots of miracles in Grandma's garden patch.

Grandma and I would stop at the newsstand to look at newspapers displayed on the rack. I would read the headlines to Grandma, sounding out the words slowly. Grandma would smile and nod to her friends who were on their way to the market. As I read to Grandma, there was a miracle in her smile, and she shared it with me and with every passerby.

Grandma and I would pass the pushcarts loaded with vegetables, fruits, and household goods on the way to the train station. We would wait hand-in-hand on the platform at the station. As the train sped noisily to a stop, it would bring a rushing wind that would make Grandma's skirt bellow out like a giant balloon. We would giggle at the image of Grandma in her puffy skirt that was reflected in the train window. Still laughing, we would board the train and take our seats by the window.

Grandma and I would watch the city slowly vanish and turn to the green stretches of countryside. The flowers had brilliant colors. The birds were flying happily. Even the rustle of the leaves in the breeze were miracles that we breathed in sweetly.

Grandma and I would get to know the ladybug that crawled on the ledge of the train window on that trip to the countryside. Grandma knew that every living thing showed its own miracles. We discovered its design, its color, its movement, and all that it wanted to show us about how unique it was as it walked along the windowsill.

We would wonder about the ladybug's family, just like Grandma wondered about the family she left behind in a country over the ocean many, many years ago. When we arrived at the countryside, Grandma would delicately place the ladybug in my hand and we would carry it off the train to a patch of flowers nearby. We would gently place it on a leaf, and hope that it would soon find a new family of its own.

At the country station, Grandma would buy me a cream soda with a nickel. Then we would walk on the dirt trail through the woods to a meadow.

Grandma would unwrap the checked cloth on the grass and we would take a long time eating the slab of kielbasa, dark bread, bunch of cherries, and chunk of cheese that we washed down with milk.

We would spread our woven shawls on the grass and lay in the sun, smelling sweet clover all around us. We would discover animal shapes in the clouds. Grandma would tell me how the birds were in a choir. I would lay in the sun listening to the miracle of the choir just like Grandma. Grandma would hum a melody and I would follow. Then together we would hum the same melody and we would join in the song around us.

We would make garlands from clover and laugh as we wrapped them around our heads. It would be quiet and peaceful in the meadow in the countryside. Grandma found miracles everywhere, and she shared them with me.

Then Grandma would take out the pad and pencil from her wicker basket. I would write each letter of her name slowly: M A R Y

Then she would try writing each letter of her name, even more slowly than I did as we sat in the meadow in the countryside with the choir of birds singing around us. I would put all the letters of her name together. Then she would do the same, more slowly and faltering until she had written her name. Her eyes would sparkle for me and for herself at the same time, and the miracle in Grandma's heart would join with the miracle in my own.

Grandma would gather up the checked cloth and the pad and pencil, and she would put them into her wicker basket. We would walk on the dirt path, turning over piles of old leaves as we walked. Grandma would point out poisonous mushrooms and edible ones. As Grandma looked at me, she would warn me in her gentle way about the dangers of poisonous mush-rooms. Then lovingly, she would point out the miracles in the texture, color, design, and shape of each mushroom. We would sniff in the musty mush-room scent and see if we could find others hiding nearby. Later, she would pick the edible ones, and I would shake dirt from the stems and place them in her basket.

Sometimes, we would pick blackberries in a clearing. I would run from bush to bush picking them by myself. We would meet together at the center of the clearing to taste the biggest ones.

Grandma and I would walk along the dirt path through the woods to a small country town and to another train station. We would stop at the country fair where there was a ferris wheel on a nearby hill. I would shiver at the sight of the carts swinging through the sky. I would fall behind and watch Grandma as she climbed in and positioned herself in one of the carts.

She would place her wicker basket on the empty seat next to her. As the ferris wheel turned around and around, Grandma's patchwork skirt would flap in the breeze. She would wave and laugh aloud as the cart swung back and forth. When the ferris wheel came to a halt, her eyes would beckon to me, and I would run to join her. I would go for my first and Grandma for her second ride on the ferris wheel. With arms embracing one another, we would feel the miracle of motion as we thrilled in riding the ferris wheel high on a hillside above the country fair.

And so, the years went by. I grew taller, probably from eating so many of Grandma's pancakes, and I became healthier, most likely from sharing in so many of Grandma's miracles.

My Grandma still had a vegetable garden that surprised us with miracles daily. I still read the headlines of newspapers to Grandma, and sometimes I even read the fine print inside.

I still helped Grandma write her name, but, after much practice, she was writing her first and her last name, too. We continued to go on outings to the countryside and for walks on the dirt path in the woods. We listened to the choir of birds and discovered animal shapes in the clouds. We ate kielbasa, dark bread, bunches of cherries, and chunks of cheese washed down with milk. We picked mushrooms and blackberries and rode the ferris wheel many times through the years with garlands of clover in our hair.

And even though Grandma has long ago passed on, Grandma and her miracles will always be present in my heart. And each new miracle that I discover will have a home there, too. To this very day, I can hear my Grandma's gentle voice saying, "Miracles can be found everywhere if you take time to find them."

Diane-Ellen McCarron

is an elementary school teacher and a parent of two grown sons. Diane-Ellen McCarron says she wrote, *Grandma's Miracles* for several reasons. First, she says she believes that children will be better able to get in touch with who they are as they read this book, and second, to recapture some of the beauty of childhood that is becoming lost. This is a true story based on the author's own relationship with her immigrant grandmother. The author says her grandmother wanted children to understand the importance of loving relationships, slowing down, simplicity, and mindful approaches to living. The author says that respect for our earth speaks for itself in this story. Ms. McCarron also believes it would be an excellent value to children who are dealing with a loss such as death or separation of a loved one.

Marilyn Lucey

currently runs Synergistic Studio, a design firm, with her photographer husband and two artistic daughters in Acton, Massachusetts. Ms. Lucey's background is in toy design for national and international companies and children's book illustration, primarily for publishers of children's educational materials.

Friends

DUSTY THE RAG

by Gina M. Pelletier

Dedicated to
My Girlies

Illustrated by Dawn Marie Pavloski

The lid opened and into the hamper dropped a sock. The sock was worn and soiled, but he was as happy as could be. This old sock hadn't seen the washer in a very long time. He couldn't wait to see his friends again.

The sock wiggled across the large hamper in search of his old friends. This was an exciting day for the sock. He could tell everyone all that he had been doing since the last time that he saw the washer.

On the other side of the hamper, the sock could see one of his dear friends, Rudy. He was a huge, white shirt that the sock remembered seeing in the hamper quite often. "Rudy?" shouted the sock. "I'm back! It is so good to see you!"

"What happened to you?" sneered the shirt as he looked at the sock in disgust.

"I have a new job now," answered the sock proudly. "It gets lonely sometimes without my match, but I have lots of fun helping to keep the house clean and tidy."

"You're a rag!" hollered Rudy. "You're a dirty, soiled, dust rag! We'll call you Dusty. Dusty the rag!" teased the shirt. The other clothes in the hamper giggled quietly.

"I thought you were my friend," whispered Dusty.

Rudy turned the other way and began laughing with the others.

Dusty couldn't find anything to say to the other clothes. He was suddenly feeling too ashamed to be around them. He slowly inched over to the other side of the hamper and began to cry. He realized that he had no friends and without his match, he wasn't even a sock. He was just a grungy, old rag.

As Dusty lay scrunched against the side of the hamper feeling lonely, the lid lifted again. A crowd of clothes came tumbling down into the hamper, landing close to the gloomy rag. Once the clothes hit the bottom, they scattered around looking for others to talk and play with.

Left behind was a tiny, beautifully colored sock. She was bright white with pink and red stripes running across her. Dusty looked at her for a moment. She was so pretty to Dusty, yet she seemed frightened and all alone. Dusty straightened himself out as best as he could and moved toward the tiny sock. "It will be all right." he said quietly. "Don't you have a match?"

"Yes I do," whimpered the sock, "but he is over there being a clown." Dusty looked across the hamper. He saw the other little pink and red sock tying himself in knots as the other clothes cheered him on.

"I don't know all of those tricks and I am very frightened of this trip to the Great Bubble Machine."

"Great it is," replied Dusty. "The Bubble Machine is wonderful and you will leave it feeling fresher and cleaner than ever before! Don't worry, I will see that you make it safely through your trip."

"Thank you so much," answered the tiny sock. "My name is Rosy, what is yours?"

"They call me Dusty," said the rag. And Dusty went on to tell Rosy how he lost his match and became a cleaning rag. He also told her about Rudy, who had teased him and had the others laughing at him too.

"He doesn't know about you!" answered an angry Rosy. "He has no match and he looks pretty dirty himself." When Dusty looked at Rudy, he saw many stains on the white shirt.

"I never noticed how dirty he was," said Dusty. "And from what I remember, he sure did make this trip a lot."

"You see?" added Rosy, "He is nothing but a big bully and you don't need him for a friend!"

The lid lifted again and most of the clothes quickly left the hamper. Rosy's match was one of the lucky ones. He was gone and Rosy was left behind with the crumpled rag. Dusty felt awful. "This is all my fault," he thought. "If she wasn't talking to me, she wouldn't be left behind now." Rosy was scared and she began to cry. "Don't worry," reminded Dusty. "I promised you that I would get you to the Bubble Machine safely, and I will."

Dusty knew he had to hurry. He told Rosy to crawl into a hole that had worn on the side of him. Now, carrying Rosy, he could get to the Bubble Machine quickly. Dusty inched as fast as he could across the floor. He could hear the water running in the distance. Could Dusty get the little sock to the washer in time?

They finally reached the room where the Great Bubble Machine stood. Dusty had to move fast, so he slinked up the side of the rumbling machine. Once at the top, Dusty let Rosy out onto the washer. "Here you go, little one." said Dusty. "You will be all right now, but you don't have much time. The lid is about to close, so you better jump in find that funny match of yours,"

Rosy looked into the big machine. She saw a sea of warm bubbles and heard a stream of laughter. It didn't seem so scary now and she was ready to jump in. "This looks like fun," said Rosy, "and I'm not afraid anymore. Don't worry what anyone says. You are a wonderful friend and you are very brave." Rosy jumped onto the fluffy pile of bubbles as the lid closed behind her.

Dusty was sad again and a tear fell from his eye. He felt alone again and that he didn't belong with the others. He remembered how Rudy had teased him. Then Dusty thought about what Rosy had said. "Why am I sad?" thought Dusty. "I made a new friend today and I did something very brave for her. No matter what anyone says, I am still special!"

When Dusty turned to climb off the washer, something caught his attention. Down behind the Great Bubble Machine lay a sock. It was covered with dust and curled up into the corner. Dusty called out to the sock. When she looked up, Dusty's face turned up into a giant smile. It was her! Dusty's match had fallen down behind the Great Bubble Machine. He quickly pulled her up to the top and tried to dust her off.

"I couldn't be a good sock without my match," she said, "so I stayed down there hoping you would find me someday."

"You're still a great sock!" answered Dusty. They both looked crumpled and dirty, but they were very happy to be together again. The two socks hugged each other tightly as they lay on the washer together waiting to be washed.

118

Gina Pelletier

is originally from New York and has resided in Texas for about 10 years. She lives there with her husband and three daughters. She is a graduate of The University of Texas at Austin. Gina has a degree in Communication Sciences and Disorders, with a focus on deaf education.

Dawn Marie Pavloski

after graduating from the American Academy of Art in Chicago with an Associates Degree in illustration and commercial art, Ms. Pavloski decided to pursue a desire by continuing her education in what she calls, the "fascinating area" of animation. She chose Columbia College to fulfill her goal, where she is finishing her Bachelors degree in Animation. Ms. Pavloski now devotes most of her time to her art and education. She enjoys exhibiting her work and finds that the charming world of children's book publishing is where she plans to keep her efforts in keen focus.

Katie Finds A Friend

by **Beth Gallagher**

*Dedicated to My Husband, Brian,
and My Mother, Nina.*

illustrated by **Maury Ann Brooks**

Katie had just moved to a new house far away from all her friends.

She was feeling very lonely because there wasn't anyone with whom she could play.

Katie missed her friends.

121

Katie's mother brought her cookies and milk to try to cheer her, but she wasn't hungry. "No thank you," she said looking at her mother sadly.

Katie's father asked if she wanted to play a game of catch with him. She loved playing sports with her father. "Maybe later, Dad," she said sadly.

Katie decided to go for a walk to see if she could find some children to play with.

She saw a group of boys in the street playing football. She ran up to them and said "Hi. My name's Katie, can I play football with you?"

"No girls allowed," one of the boys said. "Yeah!" said another.

Katie walked away and began to cry. "I hate my new house," she said.

Just then, Katie heard something behind her. She turned around and saw a black dog with white spots.

"Oh, no!" Katie screamed. Katie was very afraid of dogs. She turned and started running. The black and white dog wagged his tail and ran after her.

Katie was so frightened that she picked up a stick and threw it near the dog to scare him. The dog stopped and Katie ran home.

When Katie got home, she closed the door and started crying.

"I hate it here," she sobbed.

Just then Katie heard something at the door. She opened the door and to her surprise, there was the black and white dog, wagging his tail. In the dog's mouth was the stick that she had thrown.

The dog dropped the stick and started to lick Katie's hand. Before she
knew it, Katie was laughing and playing with the dog.

Katie's mother and father ran downstairs to investigate all the noise.

They were very happy to see Katie smiling for the first time since they
had moved.

"Can I keep him, Mom?" Katie asked.

"Well, we'll have to see if he belongs to anyone," Katie's mother answered.

Katie, her mother, and her father walked around the neighborhood to see if
they could find anyone to whom the dog belonged. They put up posters with
his picture and ran an ad in the local newspaper, but still couldn't find anyone
to whom the dog belonged.

So Katie got to keep him.

Katie and Polka-Dot became the very best of friends.

They played together every day.

And what do you think was their favorite game?

Beth Gallagher

was born in White Plains, New York, and raised in Key West, Florida. She attended the Florida State University in Tallahassee, Florida, where she received a bachelor of science degree and a master of science degree, both in Special Education. Ms. Gallagher currently resides in Boca Raton, Florida, with her husband. She teaches a Special Education class at a local elementary school.

Maury Ann Brooks

a professional artist, Ms. Brooks runs her own arts production company, Wind Pudding Productions. She studied art at Kutztown State College and after receiving a Masters Degree in painting from Hunter College in New York, she decided to pursue her interest in children's books. Making a dramatic change from large format abstract paintings, she now works with watercolor, and pen and ink on a much smaller scale. Ms. Brooks has also developed an interest in puppetry, carving several marionettes and constructing small sets using wood, wire, fabric, discarded detergent bottles, paper mache and old canvases for backdrops. She is currently working on a picture book featuring three of these puppets. Ms. Brooks has traveled in Europe, North Africa, Turkey and Alaska, and has lived in Paris for two years. She has a strong interest in nature and loves to read. Ms. Brooks lives and works in New York with her husband, a teacher.

ALLIE
AND HER NEW FRIENDS

by Nancy Boggs

Dedicated to my husband, Paul, for his everlasting love and support;
to my mom for always believing in me,
and to God who is always with me and shines His light on my road in life.

Illustrated by Michele Nidenoff

Allie is a happy little Cocker Spaniel dog. She is two and a half years old. Her fur is black and white. She lives in a nice house with her Mommy, Daddy and big brother, Max.

Allie loves to play ball with her Daddy in her back yard. Her Daddy throws the tennis ball and she runs to get it. She brings it back to him so he can throw it again.

Sometimes she plays with Max. He is a Golden Retriever. Max is 10 years old. Allie really loves Max a lot. He is just like her but he is bigger and his fur is golden instead of black and white.

Max has the tennis ball and Allie tries to take it from him. She jumps on Max trying to take the ball but he does not mind because they are just playing. Allie always has fun playing with Max. She really loves to play so she is always looking in her back yard for new friends.

Sometimes Allie gets really excited when animals and birds come in her back yard. She watches them from the window inside her house.

One day she saw a squirrel playing in her back yard. She ran to her Mommy and jumped up and down very excited asking to go outside. She wanted to run and say "hi" to her new friend. Her Mommy opened the door and Allie ran as fast as she could to meet her new friend. He saw her running quickly toward him and he was afraid. So he ran up a tree.

Every time she runs to be friends with the squirrels they run up a tree or up the fence. They do not want to be friends with Allie. They are afraid of her.

Sometimes Allie just looks out the window watching for a new friend to play with. She is sad whenever she does not see any new friends.

Finally, one day Allie saw a robin in her back yard. She was so excited to have a new friend to play with. She hoped the robin would be her friend. She ran, jumping up and down very excited, asking her Mommy if she could go outside. Her Mommy opened the door. Allie ran very fast, then started walking very slowly to get to her new friend. She did not want to scare the robin like she had scared the squirrels. She got closer - - and closer - - and closer.

The robin saw her coming and flew up on the fence before Allie could say "hi". She looked at Allie very scared and confused. She told Allie that they could not be friends because they are not alike. Allie did not understand why. She did not care that they were different. She just wanted to be friends. Allie thought they should be friends and play together even if they are different.

Allie walked back to her house. She was very sad since the robin would not be her friend.

The next day Allie was sitting in her house looking out the window. She was very sad because she wanted a new friend to play with. Suddenly, the robin landed outside the window and said "hi" to Allie. The robin told Allie that she thought about what Allie had told her the day before. She said Allie was right and that she was wrong. They can be friends even if they are different. Allie was so happy and excited to have a new friend.

She was so excited! She ran, jumping up and down, asking her Mommy if she could go outside to play with her new friend. Her Mommy opened the door and Allie ran outside to play with her new friend.

The robin tells Allie that her name is Roxy. Allie and Roxy have so much fun playing together! Sometimes Roxy flies beside Allie as she runs around in her back yard.

Then one day as Allie and Roxy are playing, Allie sees the squirrel on the fence watching them. He also changed his mind and he wants to be friends with Allie and Roxy. He slowly comes down off the fence. He says he has been watching Allie and Roxy playing together. He says his name is Scotty the squirrel. Roxy and Allie play with Scotty all afternoon. Allie is so happy to have two new friends!

Allie, Roxy and Scotty become best friends and play together every day after that day. Sometimes Max plays with them. They decide to make many other new friends too.

ALLIE'S LESSON:

You do not have to be just alike to be friends. You can play with boys or girls. And with boys and girls with different color skin. Also, with boys and girls from other countries.

Allie says "bye-bye". You are her new friend too and she loves you!

Nancy Boggs

lives wth her husband, Paul, Allie and Max, in White Plains, Maryland, about 20 miles south of Washington, D.C. Ms. Boggs works in Washington, D.C. as a manager in the computer department of the company that provides pension and health benefits for retired coal miners and their beneficiaries. She says the job is very rewarding because "The work we do makes a difference in people's lives." Ms. Boggs came from a large family and always wanted children, but never had any of her own. So, she decided to adopt a four-legged, furry, baby girl, Allie. Ms. Boggs says, " Allie is a sweet and timid

little Cocker Spaniel who is extremely devoted to her and always wants to please her. Because Ms. Boggs loves children and animals, she decided to bring them together in stories. This is the first of many stories about Allie that Ms. Boggs has written and each one presents a different lesson Ms. Boggs has also been a part-time mom to her husband's 19 year old son, Keith, whom she has known since he was two years old, and also to Erica, who came to the United States five years ago as an exchange student. Ms. Boggs also enjoys reading, photography, crafts, writing children's stories and, with her husband's help, is learning how to play golf.

Michele Nidenoff

was born August 18, 1959 in London, Ontario, Canada. At the age of five she decided she was going to be an artist when she grew up. She attended the Art Program at H.B. Beal Secondary School in Ontario, studying drawing and painting, graphic art, and animation. After graduating with a Special Art Certificate in 1977, Ms. Nidenoff worked as a graphic artist for four years for a small company in London, Ontario. In 1981 she moved to Toronto and began to work as a freelance artist, doing graphic art, illustration and calligraphy. Since 1987 her work has consisted primarily of illustration; most of which has been for children's books, magazines, anthologies and textbooks. She has also illustrated numerous stories for children's television programs on TVOntario, and last year she illustrated one of the stories in Cherubic Chidren's Story Book, Vol. One. Ms. Nidenoff, exhibits her work periodically, teaches calligraphy and occasionally does "illustrator visits" at schools and libraries.

Squish The Fish and his Neighbors

by Lynn A. Hayward

This story is dedicated to my niece Sarah with the hope that she will enjoy and learn from it. I wish her always to be open minded and to have the confidence to achieve any goal. I have all the confidence in the world in her. With all my love, "Aunt Lynnie".

Illustrated by Angie Dennis

Katt smiled and waved to Daphney and Iago. As he turned and swam away, he thought he had never felt so warm, happy and close to someone.

Katt is a fish. Daphney and Iago are chameleons. It didn't matter that they were so different. Because, they were so much alike.

143

"They weren't always my next door neighbors."

Katt was startled and stopped in mid-movement. He was a black catfish whose whiskers bristled at the interruption of his thoughts. It was out of fright more than irritation. He wasn't aware that he was being watched.

Squish's face was filled with a big smile. Once again Katt felt warm. Squish had this way about him. He made everyone around him feel loved and wanted. I am lucky! My stupid prejudice and fears almost messed this all up, Katt thought to himself.

"Daphney and Iago didn't always live next door," Squish repeated. "Before they moved here they lived out there." Squish pointed toward the window. "They lived in another building," Squish continued. "Sarah, the pretty girl that gives us food, has an aunt. 'Aunt Lynnie', that is what Sarah calls her. Shall I continue my story? " Squish asked Katt.

"Yes! Please do!" Katt eagerly answered. Squish reminded Katt of the sun. It wasn't just his yellow color. Katt swore, if you closed your eyes, you could feel the warmth exude from Squish. Just like the sun on a perfect day.

Squish continued his tale. "Once upon a time," Squish started to giggle. He was really enjoying himself. He began again. "Once upon a time, Daphney and Iago lived in another house. It was a warm house. They had a fireplace in the same room. It took away the chill of the cold, long winters. Their home was up on a shelf, but they didn't live in the big house by themselves. There were three cats.

Dusty was the older and wiser cat. His fur is spotted black and white. He has one black eye and white paws. He looks like a fighter. Squish playfully started to jab at Katt. Katt pretended to block all the blows. Their laughter made it impossible to continue. When their laughter subsided, Squish continued.

Tigger is the second oldest cat. She is a pretty cat. She has pretty, big, green eyes and she is striped. She is not to be trusted!

Phoebe is the youngest. She has light colored, short hair. She, also, is not to be trusted. She is like a kid. She doesn't realize that she is hurting you. She looks at you as a toy. It could be fatal!"

Katt suddenly felt warm breath on his shoulder. He turned his eyes, being very careful not to move his body. There was someone there. He jumped and swam right into the wall. He was dazed a little but scared a lot more. He turned to see that it was only Barney the fish. Squish was holding his stomach laughing. Barney watched Squish with a smile. He was unaware that he had helped Squish with his little joke. Barney was oblivious to a lot of things. It didn't mean that he didn't care. He was a good caring fish. He didn't have a bad word to say about anyone.

"Do you want me to continue or are you going to keep interrupting me?" Squish stared at Katt, with a sly smile.

"Continue, Mr. Comedian," Katt spit out through a smile.

"Okay, Barney you know this story. Daphney, Iago and the three cats, " Squish stated.

"Oh yes! I like Squish's stories," Barney excitedly said turning to Katt.

Squish continued on once more. "Now, you have Daphney and Iago in their home up on this wall shelf. Nobody is home except them and the three cats. Daphney is a confident and self assured type. Iago is more so now, but he wasn't always. He didn't have a lot of confidence in himself. Daphney had confidence in him and tried to encourage him whenever she could. She knew one day he would believe in himself. She just didn't realize it would be today!

Phoebe, the youngest cat, would spend every day watching Daphney and Iago. They tried to be friendly and wave to the cat. This seemed to agitate her more.

'She is starting to make me a little uneasy,' Iago whispered to Daphney.

Daphney agreed with a nod of her head. 'Maybe, I should go and talk to her. There may be a problem or maybe we just need a proper introduction, 'Daphney answered. Daphney hesitated for a minute. Her eyes looked into Iago's. They seemed to be asking him to come along. Iago just looked away. He would let Daphney handle it. He might just mess it up. That is what he had been told all his life by his parents. Iago would try and help even though he was told not to. Something always went wrong. He had gotten used to letting other people handle everything.

Iago had gotten so consumed in his own thoughts he hadn't noticed that Daphney had started over toward the cat.

Daphney would stop, smile and wave to Phoebe every few steps. Phoebe seems to be smiling, Daphney thought to herself. She continued on. With one sudden movement Phoebe had closed some distance between them. Daphney stopped. A little fear started to creep into her thoughts. Maybe, she is anxious to meet us, too, Daphney thought trying to convince herself.

With the cat's sudden movement Iago had moved further back. 'Daphney will be fine!' Iago convincingly said. He was getting so nervous that he had began talking to himself. 'The wall of the aquarium will protect her if anything goes wrong,' He continued. Iago's skin started to turn a little gray. His words were convincing, but his tone was not.

Daphney inched forward. She began to speak. 'Hi, my name is Daphney. That is Iago back there.' Daphney motioned back toward Iago never taking her eyes off Phoebe. Phoebe's eyes seemed to be getting larger. Her tail was moving at a feverish pace. She said nothing in return. Daphney tried to speak but the words wouldn't come out. She knew this was a mistake.

Suddenly, Phoebe pounced once more. She was hanging onto the aquarium. Daphney was knocked back by the impact. Phoebe let out a frightening howl as she pulled herself up to the top of the aquarium. The screen on top was partially knocked off. Daphney laid there in a daze. She was unable to move.

'Oh my gosh!' Iago screamed out. 'The cat has hurt Daphney. I must do something,' Iago cried. 'I must help her or she might die. She would do anything for me,' Iago said nervously pacing.

The thought of Daphney always telling him he could do it came to his mind. It was as if she was actually there encouraging him. 'I can do this!' Iago stated with confidence. With that, he started toward the big beast.

Phoebe was now on the top of the aquarium. She tried to squeeze her body through the small opening on top. She couldn't because the screen was only partially off. So, she stuck her paw into the aquarium. Phoebe tried to swipe at Daphney. She was just out of her reach. Phoebe stuffed her body deeper into the aquarium. The screen gave in a little. She stretched her paw toward the motionless Daphney. She could feel the lizard's body. Phoebe started to lift her from the bottom of the aquarium.

Iago smashed into the paw of the cat. With that collision Phoebe dropped Daphney. Iago hesitated only a few seconds to glance into the eyes of the big beast. They were not very happy eyes, Iago thought to himself.

'You know your breath stinks!' Iago yelled out. He was so close to the cat that he could tell what she had for lunch. With that thought Iago started heading for the opening on top. He flew right past the cat's head. They were so close that Phoebe's whiskers brushed along the back of Iago. Iago darted out the opening.

Phoebe chased after Iago. She no longer wanted Daphney. Iago dropped down from the shelf to the floor. Phoebe was in hot pursuit. Iago scurried under the couch. It slowed down Phoebe some but she continued the chase. Iago was also slowed down by this fuzzy stuff under the couch. He was still out of reach of Phoebe. Iago started up the stairs. He was on the second one when he noticed that he was being pursued by another cat.

Don't they have anything better to do with their time, Iago thought to himself.
Tigger had joined in the chase. Iago scurried up the third and last stair.
Tigger hesitated for a second and prepared to pounce on him. She jumped in
the air. Iago's back was to Tigger but he could feel her, almost on top of him.
He felt his doom! His eyes shifted above him. A spotted flash collided with
the striped shadow. Iago looked back only for a second to see that the black
and white spotted cat laid between him and the other cat. Iago scurried behind a cabinet.

Both cats stared at Dusty. Tigger picked herself off the floor. She gave Dusty a
disgusted look and started to lick her sore body. Phoebe went over to where
she saw Iago last. She could barely see Iago. The are was so small behind the
cabinet that Phoebe couldn't even squeeze her paw in. She became bored
with this and continued on to some new adventure. Tigger wasn't satisfied
with the situation and went over to the back of the cabinet to investigate.

Just then the front door opened and all three cats went to greet the visitor. It turned out to be Aunt Lynnie. She closed the door and petted all three cats. She picked up Dusty in her arms as he meowed. He continued to meow. "My Dusty you have quite a story to tell," Aunt Lynne stated. Her eyes shifted over to Daphney and Iago's home. She set Dusty down and quickly went over there. Daphney was on the bottom peering out. Iago wasn't in the aquarium! Auntie Lynnie put the screen back on tightly. She immediately knew who the culprits were.

"Tigger! Phoebe! Where is Iago? What did you do with him?" angrily she cried out. Tigger and Phoebe both averted their eyes to the floor. Dusty, who now was up the stairs, cried out. Aunt Lynnie ran to him. She could see he was looking behind the cabinet. She pushed it out a little and saw Iago. She reached in and picked him up. He was covered with dust and part of his skin was shedding. Iago was breathing very hard. Auntie Lynnie brushed the dust off him and placed him back into the aquarium. She secured the screen with some clips. Satisfied with that, she went over to talk to Tigger and Phoebe.

Daphney ran over to Iago. "Are you all right?" she asked, choking back the tears of happiness.

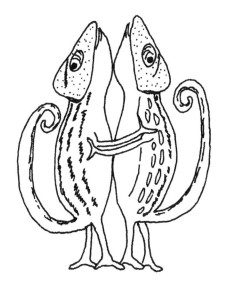

Iago squeaked out a faint "Yes. I am tired more than anything. Are you okay?" he turned his head slowly to check her out.

"I am just fine," she reassured him.

Dusty hopped up to check on his new friends. Daphney grabbed onto Iago. "It's okay! That's Dusty he helped me," Iago stated.

"Thanks Dusty!" they both chimed in together.

Dusty seemed to wink at them and hopped back down.

"You know you were great too!" Daphney amorously said.

"It's easy when I have some one like you that believes in me," Iago confidently replied.

They embraced.

Iago felt like he could do anything! Everyone that had said he couldn't, was wrong! All you have to do is give it a good try. His thoughts returned to Daphney and he hugged her closer. The End!" Squish happily shouted out.

"So Dusty is an okay cat," Katt stated. "But how did they end up over here?" Katt asked, pointing to Daphney and Iago's aquarium.

"Sarah's Auntie Lynnie moved to Florida so Sarah kept them. I hear there are a lot of relatives of Daphney and Iago there," Squish answered.

Katt, happy with his answer, swam over toward the chameleon's home. He smiled at them and turned toward Squish and Barney. "I think I am going to learn a lot from my new friends," Katt softly spoke to himself.

"All my new friends,' he confidently said turning back to Daphney and Iago. That warm feeling returned to him once again, and he swam away.

152

Lynn A. Hayward

resides and works in Brooksville, Florida. She grew up in Chittenango, New York. The author says her first published work, *Squish the Fish*, in volume one of Cherubic Children's New Classic Story Book in 1996, started an "interesting and very busy year." Besides her work as a house painter, she did many book signings and speeches. She says her talks at the elementary schools were the most fulfilling. She states, "To be able to share my story with pre-K up to fifth graders was very rewarding, not only to the children and teachers, but also to me." Ms. Hayward says "the excitement in the children's faces was contagious and overflowed to me. To be able to touch the hearts and minds of the children was very gratifying." *Squish the Fish and his Neighbors*, is her second published story. Ms. Hayward has written other stories about the adventures of Squish the Fish. Look for them in future Cherubic story book volumes.

Angie Dennis

was born in the town of Bromley, in the county of Kent, in southeast England and has been living for the past 3 1/2 years in the United States, in Lancaster, PA. She is the youngest of six children and has a twin sister. While growing up she says she felt that her family was her security blanket. And even though they are an ocean apart, she says that feeling is still with her. In England she was employed as a tracer/draftswoman, a job she thoroughly enjoyed. She and her husband, Richard, have two sons, John, age 15, and Michael, age 11. She enjoys writing as well as illustrating and has written a series of children's books about the adventures of *Alexander, the School Bear*, which she also illustrated. She says, "As a child, I was given much of the things that money can't buy; respect, honesty, trust and, above all, unconditional love." She says it is some of these values that she attempts to portray in her art and in her stories. In 1996 Ms. Dennis illustrated one of the stories in Cherubic Children's New Classic Story Book, Volume One.

Monsters

MULLIGAN AND ME

by T. J. Williams

*Dedicated to my super-amazing kids, Marie and Chris and to the one on the way.
To my wonderful husband, Vince, my favorite monster in the closet.
And, of course, to the real Alvin, my Dad.
I love you all.*

illustrated by Tom Rockwell

The night my night light went out and I was left completely in the dark, something amazing happened.

I heard someone crying.

At first I was very afraid. I pulled the covers up over my head, crawled to the bottom of my bed and hid.

It wasn't long before it was really hot under all of those covers. So, I decided to be brave. Cautiously, I sneaked out of my bed and tip-toed toward the noise.

I stopped walking and listened intently when I got to the closet doors. A big puddle of tears was rapidly growing bigger and bigger around my feet, soaking the feet of my pajamas.

I took a deep breath, reached out, flung the closet door open and jumped back!

Sitting on my closet floor, trembling among all of my toys, was a round, hairy monster!

He wasn't a very large monster. In fact, as monsters go, this was a very small monster. But, he was a monster none the less. And never having met a monster before, I wasn't sure just what to do.

So, I poked him.

The monster screamed and hid behind a bunch of wooden blocks piled in the corner of the closet. I could see his bright green eyes, as huge as saucers, staring fearfully out at me.

Crossing my legs, I sat on the floor in front of the closet.

The eyes blinked at me.

"Come on out," I said. " I promise, I don't bite."

The eyes blinked again.

"Really, there is nothing to be afraid of." I held my hands out toward the closet. "I'm just a kid. See?"

The eyes slowly moved from behind the blocks. I could see that the monster was shaking. His pink hair and purple nose quivered as he continued to stare at me.

"Maybe it will help if I introduce myself." I stood up and bowed deeply. "My name is Alvin. How do you do?"

The monster took a tiny step forward. "D-d-d-do what?" He asked.

I thought for a minute. "Well, I honestly don't know. Do anything, I guess." I shrugged.

"In that case, I do anything very carefully." He answered and took another step forward.

"Good answer. I'll remember that. Do you have a name?"

The monster scooted the rest of the way toward me and held out his hand. "I am Mulligan Monster." His stomach growled loudly.

"Mulligan, it sounds like you may be hungry. Do you wanna get a snack?"

Mulligan jumped up and down. "That would be great!"

We went into the kitchen together and turned on the light. We looked in the fridge to see what we could find.

"Oh, wow!" Said Mulligan, jumping up and down and clapping his hands. "You have salad in there! Got any Blue Cheese salad dressing? Blue Cheese is my favorite."

"Salad? Yuck! Wouldn't you rather have ice cream or candy or sweets? You know, something good."

"No, thank you," He said. "Salad is something good. It's my favorite food in the whole world! It's green and crunchy and Deeeelicious! Besides, salad makes you grow." Mulligan smacked his lips in anticipation.

"No way." I said as I dished out some salad for Mulligan. "Salad is just a bunch of lettuce, tomatoes, and stuff like that. It doesn't really make you grow. That's just one of those things grown ups say to make you eat some-thing that is supposed to be good for you."

Mulligan just smiled happily and took a huge bite. I could hear the salad crunching loudly between his teeth as he chewed. He ate until there was no more salad in his bowl. Then leaned back in his chair and sighed a very con-tented sigh.

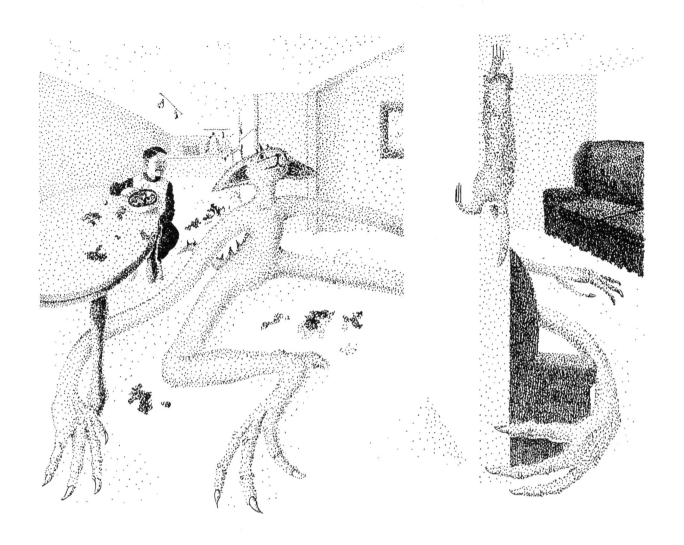

"See?" I laughed, "It's just a bunch of leaves. Salad makes you grow. Yeah, right. You are the smallest monster I've ever seen!"

I thought Mulligan was going to laugh too, but instead, he covered his mouth with his furry hand and burped. His small pink body began to shiver and shake. He was shaking all over the kitchen when he burped again. Mulligan stopped moving and I watched as his feet grew longer and longer until they almost knocked over the kitchen table.

Mulligan burped another time. This time his arms grew long and squiggly like spaghetti coming out of a spaghetti machine. They grew out the kitchen door and into the living room under Mom's big braided rug, disturbing calico, our brown and orange cat. Mulligan giggled.

Calico stalked into the kitchen and glared at us, twitching her tail irritably.

One more burp and Mulligan's body and head caught up with the rest of him, causing him to grow so much he had to scrunch himself up into a ball so his head would not go through the roof. This made Calico very angry. I don't think he likes monsters very much.

"Now what are we going to do?" I asked. "Mulligan, my mother does not allow this kind of behavior in her house. You're gonna get me grounded!"

"Quick, get me a glass of orange juice!" Mulligan demanded.

I poured some orange juice in an iced tea pitcher. A regular glass would have been too small for his huge hand.

Mulligan brought his hand in from the living room, took the pitcher and slurped the juice greedily, spilling some of it on his large, pink chest. "Ah! That's good. I just love orange juice. And it, uh oh, here we gooooooo!"

Mulligan shrank back to his normal size quickly. But there was still one little problem.

Mulligan was no longer pink. He was orange.

"Oh no! I don't want to be orange. Orange is my least favorite color in the whole world. What am I going to do?" Mulligan covered his face and cried.

Scratching my head, I thought for a minute. "Well, we know that when you swallowed something orange, your fur became orange. Maybe you can eat something pink to change you back to pink."

Looking through the refrigerator, I found broccoli, green beans and spinach which were all green.

I found yellow corn and orange carrots.

There were blue blueberries, purple eggplant, white milk and cottage cheese, and red strawberries.

"Well, I can't find anything pink. But, red strawberries are pretty close. Maybe they will do the trick." I handed Mulligan a bright red, juicy strawberry and stood back. After the salad incident, I had decided that it wouldn't hurt to be careful.

He ate the strawberry quickly, licking his fingers and smacking his lips.

Crossing my fingers and closing my eyes tightly, I hoped that Mulligan would be pink when I opened them again. But, when I opened my eyes, Mulligan had turned bright red with little black dots all over him.

"Oh, no! This is even worse! Have you ever heard of a red, polka-dotted monster? The other monsters will laugh at me. I'll be banned from all of the upcoming monster parties!" Mulligan paced back and forth in the kitchen, trying to think of a way to become pink again.

I interrupted his pacing with another idea. "At school they say that if you mix red and white it makes pink. I've never tried it. But, maybe that will work." I picked up some cottage cheese and handed it to Mulligan with a spoon. "You already ate red. Now, you just need to eat something white."

Mulligan ate a large mouthful of cottage cheese. He put down the spoon and sat very still for a moment. Then, he began to bounce. He bounced and he bounced and he bounced all over the kitchen, knocking the pot holders off the wall, turning on the water full blast, and pushing the plants over.

When he finally stopped bouncing, he had made a terrible mess.

But, he was pink again and very happy. He was so happy that he started to giggle. He giggled so much that I started to giggle, too. We giggled until we fell on the floor and rolled.

When we stopped giggling, we looked around the kitchen again. It was a complete disaster!

"Mulligan, what are we going to do? We'll never get this mess cleaned up before my parents get up."

"Do, you think they'll notice?" Mulligan asked, wide-eyed.

"Yes, of course they will notice. I don't think they'll be very happy about it, either." I answered. "We've got to fix it, fast!"

"Okay, okay," Mulligan sighed. "You go back to your bedroom and I'll take care of everything."

"You can't do all of this alone. I'll help you." I picked up a broom and started to sweep.

"No, Alvin. We'd never get it done in time. But if you leave, I can use my monster magic and it will be clean in no time." Mulligan took the broom from me. "According to Monster Code, number 503, 'No human may be present at any time monster magic is in use.' So, please, go back to your bedroom and I'll see you when I'm finished."

"Thank you, Mulligan. You're a good friend." I yawned, forgetting to cover my mouth. "I'll be waiting for you."

"You're a good friend, too, Alvin." Mulligan squeezed my shoulder and pushed me gently toward my bedroom.

In my bedroom, I crawled under my covers to wait for Mulligan. I could hear swishing noises and soft music in the kitchen as I closed my eyes to rest them for just a moment.

"Alvin, it's time to get up." Mom was standing in my doorway, smiling at me. "We're going to the zoo today. Hurry up and get dressed, sleepy-head!"

"Okay, mom." I sat up and stretched, glancing around my room.

Alone, I tumbled out of bed and searched my room for Mulligan. I looked under my bed, in my closet, in my drawers and even in my crowded toy box. I looked everywhere I could think of. Mulligan was gone. Or maybe I had just imagined him. Was Mulligan just a dream?

When I was dressed, I hurried to the kitchen for breakfast. The kitchen was perfectly neat. It looked just like it always did. But, on the kitchen table sat a small bowl of salad and a glass of orange juice.

"Do you want me to fix you some eggs for breakfast, Alvin?" Mom asked from the stove.

"No, thanks, Mom. I think I'll just have some salad." I climbed into my chair and smiled, wondering when I'd see my new friend again.

"You know, Mom, salad makes you grow."

T. J. Williams

says, "living in a chaotic home full of love and hapiness is the best inspiration for a writer." With her daughter, Marie, being what the author calls an "artistic princess," and her son, Chris, a "backhoe totin' cowboy," the author says, "life is always an adventure." Ms. Williams says being a wife and mother is what is most important to her. "But," she adds, "becoming a writer has always been a private dream." She says she never took it seriously, however. After attending three colleges, the author graduated from the University of Georgia with her B.S. in middle school education. She taught for two years, during which she married her husband, Vince, and had her first child, daughter, Marie. Ms. Williams then became a full time homemaker and began to devote more time to her writing. After a lot of encouragement from her husband, she began submitting her stories to publishers. Now, Ms. Williams' family is proud to have an author in the family. Her father, Alvin Jones, and her brother, Jeff, in Sunbury, Georgia, have been very supportive as have her mother, Peggy and her in-laws, Jim and Judy Williams in Athens, Georgia. Ms. Williams now hopes to continue her writing career. She is currently working on several other Mulligan stories and a novel.

Tom Rockwell

is a freelance illustrator from Rochester, New York. He works in a variety of media, and holds a bachelors degree in illustration, an associates degree in graphic design, and a masters degree in art education all from the Rochester Institute of Technology. In his spare time, Mr. Rockwell writes and records comedy-rap songs with his group *Sudden Death*. He also recently started a shareware company called FIDIM Interactive ("Fine! I'll do it myself!") and plans to release a series of bizarre computer games. "And," the author says, " just to make sure every last trace of sanity is drained from my skull, I also teach computer graphics at a local community college."

Mr. Rockwell's logo, and self-portrait

167

The Monster Zapper

by **Diane Nelson**

*Dedicated to
the Memory of
George "Pap Pap" Robertson*

illustrated by **Walter Storozuk**

It was a warm morning in July, the first day of Davey's visit to his grandfather's house. He dressed quickly and ran down to the porch.

"Look, Pappy. I have shoes the same as yours," said Davey to his grandfather.

Davey wore a pair of brand new, white, canvas sneakers.

169

"If you want those shoes to look like mine you'll have to put some miles on them," said Pappy. "Go inside and get your walking stick. We'll take a walk into town."

Davey had a walking stick like Pappy's. Pappy had sawed off the end of one of his old canes to shorten it for Davey. He used it whenever they took a walk together.

As they walked, Davey kicked dust onto his new shoes. Pappy chuckled.

Pappy saw their long shadows on the ground ahead. He waved his arms in the air and made a horrible sound, "Bwaaaaggghhhhh. . . ."

"Pappy. Cut that out," said Davey.

"Sorry, Kiddo," said Pappy. "Say! I've got a dollar burning a hole in my pocket. Think maybe you could help me spend it at the corner store?"

"Sure!" said Davey.

In the store, Pappy bought two cherry snow cones and handed one to Davey. They stood near the air conditioner, slurping the cool, juicy ice.

"Pappy! You're tongue's all red," laughed Davey.

"Oh, yeah? Stick out your tongue," said Pappy leaning over. "So's yours."

They walked out of the store wagging their bright red tongues at each other. They walked more slowly now. It was getting hotter.

"Let's stop in the toy store for a minute," Said Pappy.

"Yeah!" said David with a smile on his face.

Inside, Pappy picked up the Zippy Monster Zapper. "Thought maybe you could use this," he said.

"Wow! Thanks, Pappy!" Davey shouted.

Davey couldn't wait to get home and play with the Monster Zapper. "Pappy, Pappy! Please put in the batteries," he begged as soon as they got home.

Pappy sat down on the porch swing. "Let a man catch his breath!" Pappy laughed wiping his forehead with his handkerchief. "Whew!" Settling in he said, "Now let me see. The batteries go in here. Now try 'er."

Davey aimed the Monster Zapper. *FTTOINGGGG*

"Excellent," Davey said.

He played with the Monster Zapper all afternoon.

FTTOINGGGG

FTTOINGGGG

FTTOINGGGG

The Zapper was very loud but Pappy didn't mind. He was hard of hearing. Pappy lay on the hammock sipping iced tea.

Davey took aim and fired at the birdbath. *FTTOINGGGG*

"You're scaring all the birds away," said Pappy.

"Sorry," said Davey. He aimed at the trash can. *FTTOINGGGG*

Davey decided to join Pappy on the hammock.

"When you were little, were you afraid of monsters?" he asked.

"You bet," Pappy answered. "I checked under my bed every night."

"Yeah?" asked Davey. "And in the closet?"

"Yes. Definitely the closet," said Pappy.

173

After dinner, they sat in the moonlight on the front porch. It was cooler now, and the crickets chirped their summer song. "There's a lightening bug," said Pappy.

"There's another one!" Davey added. "And another one!"

Davey caught three lightening bugs. He cupped his hand and watched them glow.

After a while, Pappy said, "I think it's bedtime, Davey."

"I'm going to sleep with my Monster Zapper," Davey said as they walked to his room.

"Good idea," said Pappy with a wink.

Pappy tucked Davey in for the night. "Pleasant dreams, Kiddo," Pappy said. "Do you want me to check under your bed?"

"Yeah," answered Davey. "Are you going to check under your bed, too?"

"You bet!" Pappy said. He knelt down and looked under the bed. "All clear," he whispered to Davey.

They hugged each other.

Davey rolled over and was soon fast asleep.

In the middle of the night, a squeaky hinge awakened Davey. He sat bolt upright and noticed something pass in the hallway. He grabbed his Monster Zapper and ran to Pappy's bedroom.

Pappy wasn't in bed. Davey froze when he noticed something strange on the beside table - - a set of teeth in a jar of water. Oh, no, he thought. The monster got Pappy!

Davey crept downstairs, holding on tightly to the Monster Zapper. He tiptoed across the creaking floorboards.

Then in the shadows, a dark figure loomed in front of him. A MONSTER! Davey was shaking, but he found the "on" switch, took aim, and fired. *FTTOINGGGG*

      FTTOINGGGG

          FTTOINGGGG

              FTTOINGGGG

                  FTTOINGGGG

"Davey, Davey! It's okay. It's only me," said Pappy.

Davey squinted his eyes. "Pappy?" he asked. He ran into his grandfather's arms.

"Come here, you," Pappy said, hugging Davey. "Don't recognize me without my choppers, do you?" he asked. "Do I look scary without my teeth?"

"Nah," Davey said. "Just different."

They walked upstairs to Pappy's bedroom and sat on his bed. "I hope I didn't scare you with my Monster Zapper," Davey said.

"I'm okay now," Pappy said climbing into bed. "You were very brave and I'm proud of you.

"Thanks," said Davey. "Do you want me to check under your bed?"

"Are you going to check under your bed?" asked Pappy.

"Nah," Davey answered. As he turned to go back to his room, Davey called over his shoulder, "Night, Pappy."

Diane Nelson

born in Pittsburgh, Pennsylvania in 1952, is the eldest of eight sisters. She has fond memories of family trips to Carnegie Children's Library where she got her first library card. As a teenager, Diane was a competitive swimmer, lifeguard, and swimming instructor. College led to a bachelor's degree in Community Dietetics from Penn State University and a master's degree in Public Health Nutrition from the University of Minnesota. Diane was a nutritionist for the New York City Health Department and the Maryland State Health Department and taught Nutrition at New York University and Marymount College. She presently teaches Health and Home Career Skills in public school in Mamaroneck, New York and owns a business with one of her sisters called Classic Cakestands. She and her husband, Dave, a film producer, have two sons, Matt and Jeff.

Walter Storozuk

received his bachelor of fine arts degree from the Massachusetts College of Art, Boston Massachusetts in 1963. He started as a board artist with a small design studio which ultimately led to the position of Creative Director in Advertising with a major international corporation. He says, " The experience gave me the opportunity to hone my artistic skills, allowing me to offer a high degree of expertise to all my clients." Mr. Storozuk has offered his artistic services on a free-lance basis since first opening his studio in New York in 1985, and continues to do so in his South Florida Studio. His skills range from cartooning to realistic illustrations. Mr. Storozuk is a member of the National Cartoonists Society. A partial listing of clients includes, American Airlines, American Vision Centers, The Bradford Exchange, Crum and Forester, Entenmans, Exxon, The Historical Research Center, Inter-Governmental Philatelic Corporation, Jane Jane, Inc., Long Island Lighting Company, Michelin Tire Corporation, Most Significant Bits, Inc., Nestles, Palladium Books, R.G.M. Publications, Readers Digest, Sega of America, Romsoft, Sesame Street (CTW), Spencer Sports, Sports Centers of America, Sullivan Bluth Studios Ireland, Sunbeam, Tyndale House Publishers, United Business Institute, The Walt Disney Company, Warner Brothers, and numerous commissions for private collections.

MONSTERS NO MORE

by **Susan Buffum**

Dedicated to
Kelly Buffum

illustrated by Michele Nidenoff

My mom says that monsters only exist in my imagination. She says that I have a very vivid imagination. Now, I know that you are afraid of the monsters under your bed, and the monster in your closet, and the monster in the dark shadows of your room - - so, I want to tell you about your imagination. This is what my mom told me, and she is pretty smart!

Mom told me that I have super hero powers right inside my head!

I can conquer any monster that comes along and make it go away!

I didn't know that I had this great power until Mom said, "All kids have it,

but most don't know it's there and have no idea how to use it."

One night I was afraid of the monster under my bed.

Mom walked into my room, sat on my bed and said, "There are no real monsters. You know that. This is only an imaginary monster. He isn't under your bed at all. He is in your head. Now, your imagination is very powerful. Did you know that in your mind you can turn that monster into a potato chip? Then you just pretend that you are hungry and gobble him up, and he's gone!"

I tried it - Crunch! CRUNCH! CRUNCH!

It worked!

Another night I was afraid to go to sleep because of the monster in my closet.

Mom reminded me that there wasn't a real monster in the closet. It was just my imagination again. She said, "With your super-power mind you can change that scary ol' monster into a pretty butterfly and chase it across a big, green meadow until you are so tired that you lie down in the grass and fall asleep!"

I said the tall grass would tickle me! Mom tickled me and we laughed!

And, the monster was gone!

On another night, I was afraid of the monster in the corner who lurks in the shadows. Mom came into my room , leaned over my bed and said, "Look! Here's my little super-imaginer! What can you do to get rid of that monster tonight?" And she touched her finger to my forehead.

I thought about it for a while, then I said, "I'm going to make believe that monster is a bubble! The wind is going to blow him away. Way out over the mountains, and across the ocean, and then up to the moon!"

"There you go!" Mom said smiling at me.

I did it!

The next time I thought there was a monster in my room, I didn't have to call Mom. I wasn't afraid anymore. I knew the monster was only in my head trying to scare me.

With my super-power of imagination I could easily make him go away.

So, I turned that monster into a mouse, and I pretended that I was a cat! I chased him right out the door, and he was so scared of *ME* that he never came back! I laughed because I was so happy! Mom called, "Goodnight, sweetie-pie!"

Did you know that you have super powers, too? Try it the next time you are afraid at night, or in the dark, or when you are alone. There are no real monsters. They only exist in your imagination, and your mind is very powerful. You can turn those monsters into all kinds of silly things!

In my room there are monsters no more, only giggles!

Susan Buffum

was born in Northampton, Massachusetts, and grew up in Easthampton and Westfield, Massachusetts. She graduated from Westfield State College with a Bachelor of Science Degree in Criminal Justice. Ms. Buffum has worked in the criminal justice field as a store detective/assistant security manager, a Campus Police Officer and as a Campus Police Supervisor. She most recently worked as a toymaker for a major construction toy company in Enfield, Connecticut. She left that job in 1991, one month before her daughter was born, and has not yet returned to the work force. She firmly believes her full-time job is to raise her daughter and not trust that important responsibility to others. She says "I have not regretted my decision, and the benefits have been incredible!" Ms. Buffum is active in the Papermill Elementary School Parent Teacher

Organization (P.T.O). Her other hobbies and interests include reading, teddy bear & vintage Barbie doll collecting, photography, pen & ink drawing, rock & mineral collecting and cats. Ms. Buffum currently resides in Westfield, Massachusetts with her husband, John, their daughter, Kelly, and their wonderful adopted stray cat, Marty.

Michele Nidenoff

was born August 18, 1959 in London, Ontario, Canada. At the age of five she decided she was going to be an artist when she grew up. She attended the Art Program at H.B. Beal Secondary School in Ontario, studying drawing and painting, graphic art, and animation. After graduating with a Special Art Certificate in 1977, Ms. Nidenoff worked as a graphic artist for four years for a small company in London, Ontario. In 1981 Ms. Nidenoff moved to Toronto and began to work as a freelance artist, doing graphic art, illustration and calligraphy. Since 1987 her work has consisted primarily of illustrations for children's books, magazines, anthologies and textbooks. She has also illustrated numerous stories for children's television programs on TVOntario. Last year she illustrated a story in Cherubic Children's New Classic Story Book, Volume One. She has illustrated two stories in this, Volume Two. Ms. Nidenoff, who exhibits her work periodically, teaches calligraphy and occasionally does "illustrator visits" at schools and libraries.

Nature

The Deadest Fish in all the Sea

by Mare Freed

Dedicated to Dad
who parodied everything, and would have
been merciless with this story.

illustrated by Eleanor Knapp Walsh

The word went out in ebbs and tides,

in oceans, bays and water slides;

a contest seeing who could be
The Deadest Fish In All The Sea!

Murky rumors did abound;

the deadest fish would soon be
crowned!
Each dead fish thought secretly,
"There is no fish as dead as me!

Dead fish left their muddy banks,
their foamy floats and septic tanks.
They rode the waves as day drew dim
(for they were dead and couldn't swim).

None the deader for the trip
they gathered near a sunken ship.
Lobsters hailed a welcome call
to dead contestants, one and all!

Fish deceased for months and weeks,
battered by the seagulls' beaks.
Popping eyes and dropping scales,
Missing heads and missing tails.

Fish from Spain and Singapore
graciously expelling gore.
Fish from San Francisco Bay
dragging seaweed all the way.

194

Mackerel sporting swallowed hooks.
Minnows fried by Chinese cooks.
Seven crispy cod croquettes.
Twenty tuna in a net.

Cans releasing dead sardines.
Angler fish with bursted spleens.
Whitefish turned a shade of blue.
Catfish whose nine lives were through.

Halibut and rainbow trout
with their bellies bloating out.
Flattened guppies hid beneath
piles of dead piranha teeth.

Sunfish spotted with disease.
Goldfish flushed down lavatries.
Some in states of deep decay,
others dead just yesterday...

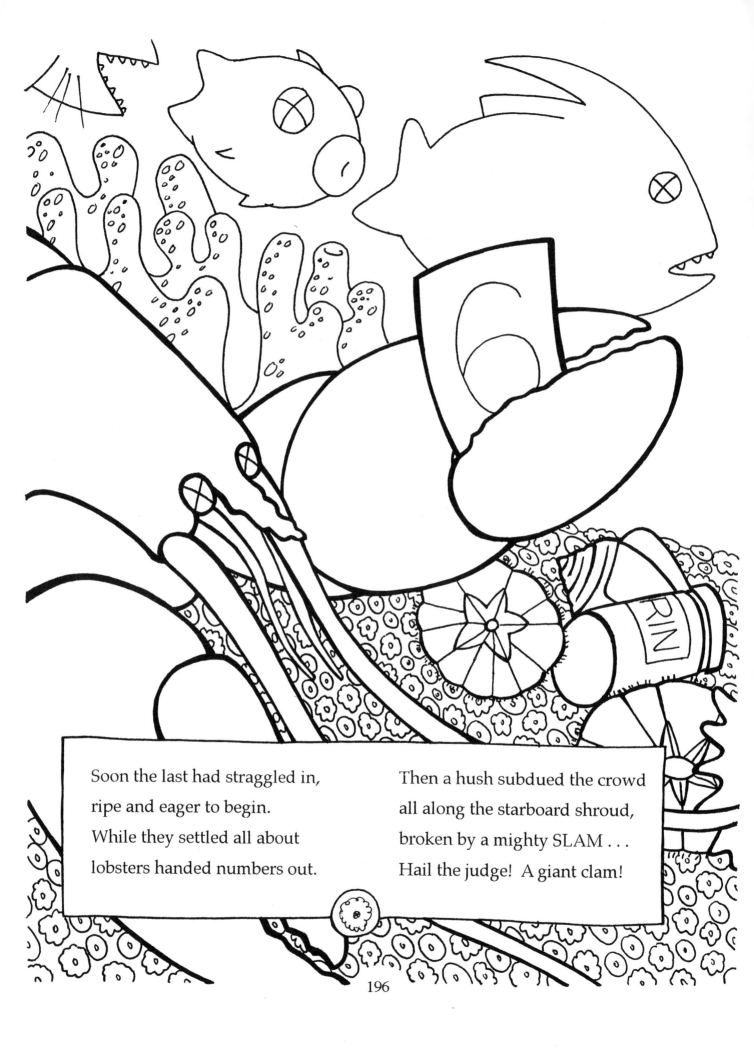

Soon the last had straggled in,
ripe and eager to begin.
While they settled all about
lobsters handed numbers out.

Then a hush subdued the crowd
all along the starboard shroud,
broken by a mighty SLAM . . .
Hail the judge! A giant clam!

Competition mounted thick.
Dead fish topped each other's tricks.
Showing off their dead fish skills:
sinking, floating, lying still.

Mobs of urchins got in tiffs
betting on their favorite stiffs.
Who would claim it? Who would be
The Deadest Fish in All the Sea?

Like a lofty magistrate
the clam observed in silent state.
Spitting out a rusty can,
he sighed a sigh and then began...

"I'm to choose the honoree,
The Deadest Fish in All the Sea.
Though I've judged the oceans' best
watching this, I must protest!"

Eyes were on him, hard and long.
Scandal! Outrage! Something's wrong!
Then the ancient clam commenced;
"Has the whole world lost it's sense?!"

"Many moons and stars ago
currents of the sea would flow
brilliant blue the world across.
Through the waves the fish would toss.

Fish alive! Robust and strong!
Full of life and sport and song.
Sea to sea and deep to deep,
multitudes of fish would leap!

By the plankton on my shell,
I recall their revels well.
Fish would travel to compete
here before my judge's seat.

I would crown the brightest tail,
highest jump and smoothest sail.
Lively contests every day
far ago and long away.
BUT...

Now we're here, oh friends of mine,
soaking in the filthy brine.
Not in all my hundred years
has a contest wrung such tears."

"Tell us why we all are dead,"
said a barracuda head.
"Aah," the clam moaned wistfully,
"Look around, it's plain to see.

This I tell you with a frown;
PEOPLE turned the waters brown!
Spilling sewage in the tide,
where were all the fish to hide?

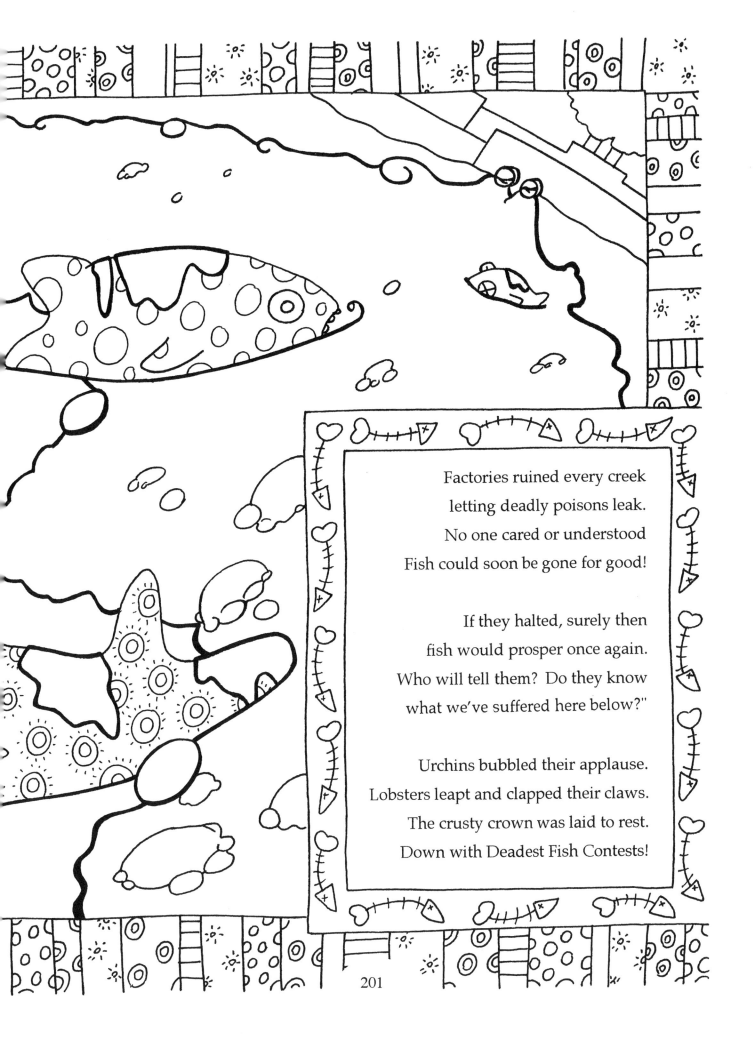

Factories ruined every creek
letting deadly poisons leak.
No one cared or understood
Fish could soon be gone for good!

If they halted, surely then
fish would prosper once again.
Who will tell them? Do they know
what we've suffered here below?"

Urchins bubbled their applause.
Lobsters leapt and clapped their claws.
The crusty crown was laid to rest.
Down with Deadest Fish Contests!

THEN...

One by one and two by two
the dead fish knew just what to do.
Ten by ten and thousands more
they washed themselves upon the
shore.

To the corners of the earth;
Baffin Island, Nome and Perth,
Boston Harbor, Shanghai Beach,
anywhere the tide could reach.

There they rested on the sand
where the water met the land,
as a message lying there
to the people everywhere.

There they lie this very morn
and as newer fish are born,
Share their message with a
friend...

Make the waters clean again.

Mare Freed

born in 1963, is a native of Cleveland who was relocated as a 1970's adolescent to Rochester, N.Y. A writer of plays, fiction, and occasional poetry, her work has been published in *HazMat Review, Hotel Dire, The Boston Poet, Daka Magazine,* and *The Upstate Writers Poem-A-Day Calendar.* She has written four plays, including *Protection,* which was produced at W.O.W. Cafe Theatre in NYC, and *Your Own Personal Savior,* which has been featured at the Boston Center for the Arts in December 1996. Her other stage works have been produced at the Cleveland Public Theatre (The Cleveland Performance Festival), Hall Walls of Buffalo, and Pyramid Arts Center. Her chapbook, also titled *Protectron,* is part of the University of Rochester's permanent collection of artist books on display in the library's museum. She now lives outside of Boston, where currently she is working on a documentation of her great-grandmother's Jewish immigrant experience.

Eleanor Knapp-Walsh

grew up near the famed celery fields of Sarasota, Florida. Torn between the lure of deep sea fishig and her love of art, she attended Ringling School of Art and Design as an illustration major (only a couple minutes walk to the Gulf of Mexico). After attaining her BFA she traded her warm coastline for the waters of Pittsburgh's three rivers. There she resides, drawing and painting, with her mischievous kitty, Murphy, and her husband, Michael, who has yet to convince her that three rivers are better than one big gulf.

Freddy Fluff
and
Mrs. Benton's Birds

by Greg Brooks

*Dedicated to My Grandparents,
William and Charlotte,
and to Freddy Fluff.*

illustrated by Adam Wallenta

It was a warm, lazy summer morning in late June. Sunshine sparkled on the bay, and a salty breeze rustled the leaves on the old mulberry tree in Freddy Fluff's front yard.

Freddy Fluff is a Maine Coon cat with long, fluffy hair. He lives in a big, two-story house by the bay with his people, Charlotte and William. Freddy decides to take a nap on the old wooden chair down by the bay. Freddy loves napping in his chair. He also loves the bay and watching sailboats whisk back and forth across the water on sunny days like today. The sunshine warms his fur and the salty air tickles his nose.

Just as he is settling down for his nap, Freddy hears a familiar voice call his name.

"Good-bye, Freddy Fluff!" Charlotte calls from the driveway. Charlotte is wearing a crisp, white nurse's uniform and white shoes. She works at the local hospital.

Freddy trots across the yard. He rubs up against Charlotte's legs and purrs.

"Have fun and be a good kitty," Charlotte tells Freddy with a smile.

Then she wags her finger at him and says firmly, "But do not go into Mrs. Benton's yard!"

Charlotte gets into her car, waves to Freddy, and drives off to work.

Then Freddy hears another familiar voice.

"Good-bye, Freddy Fluff!" William calls. William is wearing a soft, white shirt with a purple tie and dark blue dress pants. He works at a company that makes medicine for people.

Freddy trots over to William. He rubs up against William's legs and purrs.

"Have fun and be a good kitty," William tells Freddy with a smile.

Then he wags his finger at him and says firmly, "But do not go into Mrs. Benton's yard!"

William gets into his truck, waves to Freddy, and drives off to work.

Freddy was on his own. He thought how fun it would be to chase birds in Mrs. Benton's yard. Freddy likes chasing birds. Tall birds. Small birds. Fat birds. Thin birds. Freddy likes chasing them all.

Right in the middle of Mrs. Benton's yard stood a gigantic bird bath and a tall bird feeder, both teeming with birds! Birds just waiting to be chased, Freddy thought.

Freddy Fluff knows Mrs. Benton likes birds. But she doesn't chase them. Every morning hundreds of birds fly into her yard for breakfast and a bath. Mrs. Benton sits on her front porch and talks to her friends the birds as they eat and bathe.

"Good morning, Tom! Good morning, Frances!" she calls to them.

The birds chirp a happy song in reply.

Freddy Fluff knows Mrs. Benton does not like cats; any kind of cat. Mrs. Benton yells whenever she spots Freddy in her yard.

"Get out! Get out, you pesky cat! Leave my birds alone!"

She waves an old broom at him that she keeps on her front porch. She promises to swat cats with the broom if she catches them. But Freddy can run faster than Mrs. Benton. So he gets away.

Freddy Fluff stares through the fence that divides the two yards.

He stares past the roses, hollyhocks, and periwinkles growing in Mrs. Benton's flower garden.

He stares past the tomatoes, peppers and lettuce growing in her vegetable garden.

Hundreds of birds are eating and bathing right before his eyes, just waiting to be chased.

Then Freddy Fluff remembers the warning from Charlotte and William.
Do not go into Mrs. Benton's yard.

"It can't hurt to look," Freddy Fluff says.
So he sneaks carefully and quietly across his yard.
He hides behind the huge oak tree near the fence and peers
into Mrs. Benton's yard.

Mrs. Benton is not on the porch.

"Perfect!" Freddy whispers with excitement. "Now is my chance!"

So, despite the warning from Charlotte and William, Freddy Fluff
slowly slithers through a small opening in the fence and makes his
way into Mrs. Benton's yard. He stays close to the ground and keeps
his eyes on the birds.

210

He creeps closer and closer to the birds.

He sneaks past the tomatoes.

He inches past the peppers.

He slinks past the lettuce.

He sneaks past the roses.

He inches past the hollyhocks.

He slinks past the periwinkles.

Closer and closer he crawls. Freddy gets ready to pounce on a finch near the bird bath when suddenly he hears . . .

WOOF WOOF! WOOF!

A towering German Shepherd appears from the other side of Mrs. Benton's house and runs straight toward Freddy!

WOOF WOOF! WOOF!

Freddy Fluff's hair stands on end.

He rockets back to the fence as fast as his legs will carry him.

"Run faster, legs!" Freddy begs his legs.

He bolts past the periwinkles, dashes past the hollyhocks, sprints past the roses. He bolts past the lettuce, dashes past the peppers, and sprints past the tomatoes.

Finally, Freddy
reaches the fence.
He slithers through
the small opening, races
across his yard and shoots up the
trunk of the Mulberry tree.

The dog runs up to the fence. It stands guard and
barks at poor Freddy Fluff. Freddy huffs and puffs and glares
down at the dog with a frown.

Mrs. Benton appears on the front porch. She looks up at Freddy
with a wide grin. "I see you have met Daisy."

Daisy stops barking and joins Mrs. Benton on the porch.

Freddy glares down at Mrs. Benton with the same frown.

Birds now return to the feeder and the bath basin. Still smiling,
Mrs. Benton sits on her chair and talks with her birds as they eat
and bathe.

Daisy lays down next to Mrs. Benton and
goes to sleep.

Freddy notices
that Mrs. Benton's
old broom is
missing from
its spot on the
porch.

She does not
need the broom
now that she has
Daisy, Freddy thinks.

After all that running and the scare he just had, Freddy is very tired. He climbs down the tree and runs over to the wooden chair down by the bay. He jumps up and gets cozy. Soon Freddy is fast asleep.

He dreams about Charlotte and William. He remembers how they wagged their fingers at him and warned him, *Do not go into Mrs. Benton's yard.*

They knew it wasn't safe. They knew Freddy had no business chasing Mrs. Benton's birds.

But Freddy had not listened to them. He had chased the birds anyway. And what had happened? He had gotten into trouble. He had chased the birds and then Daisy had chased him. Freddy did not like being chased by the dog. Daisy had scared him. Freddy wondered if the birds were scared when he chased them. That doesn't feel good, Freddy thought.

The dream repeated itself over and over in Freddy's mind. Charlotte and William wag their fingers at Freddy. Then Freddy chases the birds and Daisy chases Freddy. After the fifth time through the dream, Freddy suddenly awakened. He knows what the dream has been trying to teach him.

Daisy scared me just like I scared the birds. If I don't want to be frightened, then I shouldn't frighten others. I should listen to what Charlotte and William tell me. They care about me and want me to be safe.

Freddy spends the rest of the day napping and playing in his own yard. Freddy decides for sure never to go into Mrs. Benton's yard again. That night, when Charlotte and William return home from work, Freddy rubs up against their legs and purrs.

He has learned his lesson.

Gregory W. Brooks

is a doctoral student in the Department of Reading, University of New York at Albany and a research associate with the National Research Center on English Learning and Achievement there. He holds teaching licenses in elementary education and reading, serves as an educational consultant, and is vice-president of his local reading council. This is Mr. Brooks' first published children's story. The author says, "Freddy Fluff was one of six curious cats from my childhood who loved chasing birds with his brothers and sisters and getting into other mischief." Mr. Brooks is currently writing other *Freddy Fluff*

adventures with the assistance of his cat, Boots. He lives near Albany, New York.

Adam Wallenta

is an illustrator living in Willimantict, Connecticut, with his art studio in Stratford, Connecticut. He says his objective as an illustrator is "to work professionally in all fields and never stop learning." He has a B.F.A. degree in communication design and illustration, is a graduate of Pratt Institute with honors, and is computer literate in Macintosh programs. His art includes oil and water colors, black and white pen and ink, and sequential art and story telling. To his credit are covers for the magazines, *America* (January 1997) and *True West* (April 1997), and text illustrations for the *American Adventures* children's book series #1-48 from Barbour and Company (1997), and cartoonist for Marvel Comics since 1994. Mr. Wallenta also was the illustrator for a *DUNE* collectible game card for Last Unicorn (1997).

The Frog Croaked at Midnight

by Pahl W. Rice

*Dedicated to my three frog watchers
Drew, Nathan, and Zachary.*

illustrated by Jeannie Hamilton

A long time ago, on a large, quiet, country pond lived a frog.
The frog's name was REE DEEP.

REE DEEP enjoyed living on the pond very much. On the tranquil,
sunny afternoons he would sit on the big lily pads and sun himself,
while he feasted on mosquitoes.

On the rainy days, he relaxed under the broad leaves of the plants that grew along the edge of the pond. Quietly, he would gaze out on the pond and watch as the droplets of rain playfully danced on the water.

At night, he would hide under the water with only his eyes showing above the surface. He would stare up at all the beautiful stars in the sky, and eat any of the unwary fireflies that passed by.

During the summer he enjoyed swimming with the turtles (they were slower than the fish and easier to keep up with). But you had to be careful of the snapping turtles. They would try to bite your toes while you swam.

Sometimes, while sunning themselves, the turtles would line up and let him play leap frog. REE DEEP stayed dry jumping from one turtle shell to the next. They all enjoyed that game.

Although REE DEEP enjoyed all this, he still felt a bit lonely. He wanted other frogs to play with, share stories with, and eat all the bugs with.

So, one afternoon, REE DEEP set out around the pond to see if there were other frogs he could befriend.

Soon, he met many other frogs who also lived on the pond. As he met them he would invite them back to his home. After a while, many of the frogs on the pond were coming to REE DEEP's house. They were having so much fun that they started bringing their friends along.

Now, there were all kinds of frogs getting together each night at REE DEEP's house, to play, dance, sing, tell stories, and share all the mosquitoes, gnats and other bugs flying around the pond.

Unfortunately, a problem arose. The frogs found it difficult to travel such a long way each night to get together. They didn't know what to do, because they still wanted to get together to have fun.

Well, REE DEEP was also a pretty clever frog. After some thought, he called all the frogs together. "Wait until after dark, when it is quiet over all the pond," he said. "Then, instead of all coming here, we can call each other over the water," REE DEEP told them with a smile on his face.

So, the next night, after dark, many of the frogs came to the edge of the pond to see if anything was going on. They were a little disappointed because it was still very quiet. One of them decided to see if REE DEEP was on the other side waiting. So, he started calling out "REE DEEP - - REE DEEP."

REE DEEP responded to the call and soon all kinds of frog noises could be heard. You could hear frogs singing and dancing, frogs calling out stories and telling jokes across the water. The fun and games continued without all the traveling. They all enjoyed themselves on the pond, because any of them could join in.

Even to this day, when the sun sets, you can go out to the pond and listen to the frogs as they come out to play. You can even hear the frogs calling out for their old friend - - REE-DEEP, REE-DEEP, REE-DEEP.

Pahl W. Rice

quotes Charles Darwin as saying, "I shall always feel respect for every one who has written a book, let it be what it may, for I had no idea of the trouble, which trying to write common English could cost one." Mr. Rice says, "I have experienced both the joy and anguish of writing, in the process of doing this story." He says, "As my first published work, I had no idea what was involved, from writing the story to seeing it published in a book." The author adds, "I hope all who read this story will enjoy it, experience it, and share it. The story came from the heart, composed for my children, and inspired by the lake we live on."

Jeannie Hamilton

was born and raised in Meriden, Connecticut, where she lives today. She says she was "born with a pencil in my hand and raised in an artis-tic family where drawing and creativity were always present and encouraged." Her father is an excellent artist and her grandfather was a very popular architect in Connecticut. As a child, Ms. Hamilton says she "took a great interest in my grand-father's talents, and would pour over his old drawings for hours, admiring his unique style and flair for artistic expression." She later earned an Associates Degree in Architechtural Engineering, and began her pro-fessional career working for a civil engineering firm drawing site plans, topographical maps, and detailed schematic renderings for presen-tations and job proposals. Ms. Hamilton is presently employed as Head Draftsperson for the City of Meriden Engineering Department. Ms. Hamilton also does freelance work in the graphic arts field designing logos, wedding invitations, all-occasion cards, book and pam-phlet illustration as well as sign carving and the design and manufacture of her own sterling silver jewelry line, Silverpaws.© She has illustrated two books on decoy and fish carving, as well as stories and product advertisements. She illustrated a story her brother wrote in Cherubic Children's New Classic Story Book, Vol. 1, and served as an art consultant in this volume. When she is not working, she likes to spend time with her family, which includes her two horses, Stormy and Jeramia.

Self Esteem

BECAUSE

I AM

by Carla O'Brien

Dedicated to My Special Ones,
Cullen and Cassidy

illustrated by Micah Hayes

"Your coloring's so beautiful," I told my son one day,
"So lively and unusual, it beckons us to play."

227

"You're talented and gifted; an artist sure to be."

"But why?" I asked sincerely, a mother's gentle plea.
The answer came quite simply,
"Because I am, you see."

"I see you helped your sister," I told my son one day.
"You made me smile. You held her hand and helped her on her way."
"You're sweet, kind and loving, a mother's dream come true.

"But why?" I asked sincerely, a mother's gentle plea.
The answer came quite simply,
"Because I am, you see."

229

"I heard you singing in the tub," I told my son last night.
"It sounded great! You made me laugh. I held my belly tight."
"You're quite a jolly singer. Your confidence shines through."

"But why?" I asked sincerely, a mother's gentle plea.
The answer came quite simply,
"Because I am, you see."

230

"I saw you hit the baseball," I told my son today.
"It went so far and high, it flew a mile, I'd say."
"You're such a good team player, the coach says you're the best."

"But why?" I asked sincerely, a mother's gentle plea.
The answer came quite simply,
"Because I am, you see."

"I watched you sleeping in your bed," I told my son today.
"It gave me goosebumps on my skin, you looked so sweet that way."
There's only one like you, you know, a special one to me."

"But why?" he asked sincerely, a young boy's gentle plea.
The answer came quite simply.
"Because you are, you see."

Carla O'Brien

grew up in the rolling hills of Northeast Iowa where she credits her fifth grade teacher for inspiring her to begin her writing career. She says her "passion for literature and writing has blossomed through the years, primarily focusing on children's books." She adds that she shares this love with her two children, Cullen, 6, and Cassidy, 2, and is supported enthusiastically by her husband, Patrick. Ms. O'Brien resides in Tampa, Florida, where she is a singer/songwriter with the contemporary Christian group, *HeartSong*.

Micah Hays

is a rising new talent who made his professional debut with his comic strip "Zoology" that ran for nearly three years. He went on to "cartoon college," a weekly cartoon strip distributed to over forty newspapers across the country by United Features Syndicate. He has since accepted commissions from such noted companies as T.G.I. Friday's, O'Charleys, and the General Electric Company. Mr. Hays graduated from Transylvania University - that's right, Transylvania U, in his home town of Lexington, Kentucky, where he studied under the renowned Kentucky artist, Joseph Petro. Last year Mr. Hays illustrated two stories in Cherubic Children's New Classic Storybook, Volume One. He lived for a short time in New York and Rhode Island, but currently Mr. Hays lives and works in Eldridge, Maryland.

The Balding Eagle

by H. Chip Zyvoloski

*Dedicated to Gay, Lane, Sean, Mom and Dad,
with special thanks to Dave M.*

illustrated by Angelo Lopez

Ed watched his reflection as he soared out over the glassy water.

And he liked it.

In it he could see his dark brown head and body. He could see the broad span of his mighty wings and his golden feet with their strong, sharp claws.

Ed hunted and fished from up there, too. If a fish swam into his reflection, Ed would drop down from the sky and snatch it right out of the water! Birds and animals scattered in fear when they saw him hunting from the sky.

When he wasn't flying, Ed perched near his nest in the tallest tree. From up there he could see all the world - - and all the world could see him. Sometimes he just had to puff out his chest.

He was a proud, young eagle!

Then one day as he soared over the water, Ed noticed something different about his reflection. He had white spots on his head and neck. "EEEEEEK!" he screeched. "Could that be me?"

Ed dove from the sky to the nearby shore, hopping to the edge of the water for a closer look. He stared at his reflection, twisting and straining to see every tuft of white on his head and neck. " How can this happen?" he wondered. "I'm an EAGLE! I don't want to change."

He leaned out over the water again for another look. "Stop that!" he squawked to his reflection. "Stop that right now!"

But squawking didn't make the white spots go away.

Ed fought back tears. "But I don't want to change," he complained to his reflection. "I want to stay just the way I am - - with a *brown* head."

Ed stared into the water for a long time. How could he keep from changing? Then it came to him, "I'll just pluck out the white feathers!"

Ed wobbled on one foot as he tried to pull out little white feathers with the other. "Aawk!" he cried each time he plucked one out. "Aawk! Aawk! Aawk!" he shrieked, as he lost his balance and fell over.

"Oh, it's no use," he cried as he flopped on the weedy beach. "I'll never be able to pull them all out!"

But as he got back on his feet, he thought of *another* plan.

Ed balanced again on one foot, carefully combing the brown feathers with his mighty talons. It took a long time, but it worked - - almost all the white was covered.

"Hello there, you handsome young eagle," he boasted to his reflection when he finished. But as he bragged, a gust of wind blew the feathers off the white spots and into his eyes. He fell beak-first into the water!

Ed flapped and sputtered on the shore as he got back on his feet. "Oh, that's not going to work, either," he squawked, spitting out sand and weeds.

Ed slowly leaned out over the water to see himself again. He was wet and muddy and out of ideas. "I don't want to change," he cried. But to his surprise, his head was *brown* again! A drippy, brown lake weed was on his head!

The weed covered almost all the white spots. It was just the right color brown. And when Ed slouched over, tucking in his beak just the right way, he could hide the rest of the white on his neck!

Ed stood at the water's edge for a long time admiring himself. Tucking in his beak that way hurt, but it was worth it. He looked like a mighty young eagle again!

Ed spread his wings, springing into flight with a new confidence. But as he flapped his wings, the weed began sliding off his head. "EEEEEEK!" he called as it dropped into the water below.

Ed dove down to the water and gently lifted out the precious weed. On shore, he carefully placed it back on his head. It was soggy and torn. Water dripped from the weed into his eyes. But he looked *young!*

Ed tried again and again to fly with the weed cap, but it slipped off every time. And every time he picked it up, the weed was a little soggier and a little more torn. Finally, Ed realized that to look young, he would have to stop flying.

So he did.

But life without flying wasn't as easy as Ed expected. He couldn't get up to his nest in the tallest tree. He couldn't soar out over the water to look at his reflection. He couldn't snatch fish out of the water for food. Instead, Ed slept in the bushes near the lake shore. He chased after small animals to eat, but they were too fast for him. So he ate seeds and berries like a small bird.

Many days passed. The lake weed on his head became dry and flaky. All the walking made Ed tired. His neck hurt from trying to balance the weed and hide the white on his neck. He was getting tired of eating only seeds and berries, too. *But at least he looked young!*

As he slowly scratched his way through the underbrush, Ed came upon a large bush with juicy red berries. A group of small sparrows filled the bush, eating and chattering as they hopped from one twig to another. Usually, little sparrows flew away when they saw a mighty eagle. But they didn't fly when they saw Ed.

"Little birds! Drop some berries down here for me!" he ordered.

"We don't want to share our berries with an old hen like *you*," snipped one of the birds.

"Old hen?" replied Ed. "I'm not an old hen!" He puffed out his chest, but that made the weed start to slide off his head, so he quickly slouched back over. "Can't you see? I am a proud, young eagle," he peeped.

The sparrows all chirped with laughter. "Eagles don't walk on the ground eating berries!" one called down to him.

"They live in the sky and eat fish that they snatch out of the water," scoffed another.

"You are not an eagle. You are an old hen." The sparrows all chirped again and went back to their eating.

"But I *am* an eagle," Ed reminded himself. "Even if my looks change. Even if I get older. I will always be an EAGLE!"

Ed looked up at the sparrows eating their berries. *He didn't even like berries.*

He looked down at his tail feathers, dragging on the ground. He looked at his feet and talons, scratched and dirty. *He hated living on the ground!*

With a mighty leap, Ed lifted up off the ground, taking flight, "I AM AN EAGLE!" he screeched as he flew over the bush. The startled sparrows scattered in fear.

As Ed flapped his wings, the dried, brown lake weed blew off his head. But this time he just let it fall. He did not want it anymore. Ed watched as the weed plopped into the calm water below, sending ripples through his reflection. In it he saw a mighty eagle with a *white* head and a *white* tail.

And he liked it.

Ed soared in the sky admiring his new reflection for hours. He snatched fish from the water with his mighty claws. And at the end of the day, Ed sat in his nest at the top of the tallest tree. From up there he could see all the world - - and all the world could see him.

He puffed out his chest.

He was a proud, *bald* eagle.

244

H. Chip Zyvoloski

lives in Sauk Rapids, Minnesota, with his wife and two children. Like the eagle in his story, Mr. Zyvoloski says his appearance has changed in the last 36 years. He says he "grew from an infant into a 5-foot-10-inch tall man, gaining more than 160 pounds in the process, lost all my baby teeth, my hairline is receding a bit and the hairs that remain are turning prematurely gray. And that's okay." Mr. Zyvolski received a bachelor of arts degree in political science from Hamline University, St. Paul, Minnesota, and a juris doctor degree from the University of Minnesota Law School. He creates forms and other products for a national company that serves the financial services industry. He insists that his job "is more exciting than it sounds."

Angelo Lopez

was born to a navy family in Norfolk Virginia. He says he has loved creating art since he was a young child. Mr. Lopez graduated from San Jose State University with a degree in Illustration, and since that time he has pursued a freelance illustration career. When he is not painting, Mr. Lopez is either reading, playing basketball, or watching old movies. He currently resides in San Jose, California.

Rupert's Gift

by John McCarthy

*Dedicated to My Parents for teaching me self-esteem,
My Wife for her encouragement,
and my Little One who will learn an appreciation
for Blue Jays and Butterflies.*

illustrated by Miriam Sagasti

Rupert wanted a friend.

With wings spread, he soared above evergreens blanketed in snow, and trees that reached with bare limbs to the sky. Rupert had beautiful shades of blue feathers that ruffled in the cold breeze.

247

Since leaving his mother's nest, he'd been lonely.

Blue jays had a reputation of being bullies, and other birds left them alone.
Rupert was always kind and friendly. But, other birds saw only a blue jay.
He landed on the roof of an isolated cabin. He wanted so much to be accepted
by other birds.

"Help!"

Rupert looked for the distant voice, but saw no one.

"Help me! I'm in the chimney," the voice screeched.

Rupert fluttered to the lip of the chimney. The smoke made it difficult to see
or breathe. "Who are you?" Rupert whistled.

"I'm a caterpillar - - can't get - - out," the caterpillar gasped between coughs. "Help me - - hard to breathe."

Rupert took a deep breath and flapped down the chimney. His eyes stung from the blinding smoke but he followed the caterpillar's coughs. Gently grasping the caterpillar in his beak, he fluttered out. On the roof they sucked in the sweet, pure air.

The caterpillar was plump and gray. "Thank you. My name is Aura," the caterpillar said. "I will grant you a gift."

"You don't have to give me anything," Rupert said. "I did what anyone should." Soot drifted everywhere as Rupert shook his feathers.

"Oh, no," she said. "I would have died if not for you. Please let me show my gratitude."

Not wanting to hurt Aura's feelings, Rupert agreed. "Could you make me black like this soot?"

Aura frowned. "I can, but why? You're nice the way you are."

Rupert explained how if he were a different color, maybe other birds would play with him. Aura's frown deepened, but she agreed to help. She spun silky black strings and placed them across his back. The silk glowed dark blue and melted into his feathers turning them black.

"Your feathers will stay black until water touches your back," Aura told him.

"Oh, thank you." Rupert squawked. "I can't wait to see the other birds!" With that, he soared off the roof.

Aura shouted, "I'll be here, if you change your mind."

As the snow melted, Rupert lived with the birds at the Twin Pines Nature Center. Among the pines and evergreens, there were many hanging feeders. In the center, water bubbled over carefully stacked rocks into a bird bath. The birds were friendly and invited Rupert to play with them. Sometimes he wondered if they'd like him without his disguise.

One day, Rupert saw a blue jay eating alone from a feeder. "Hey," he said to his companions, "What if one of us was a blue jay? We'd still be friends, right?"

The birds whistled with laughter. "Oh, Rupert! You're so funny."

"I'd never be friends with a blue jay," said a rose breasted grosbeak who always spoke fast. "They're so mean." The others nodded in agreement.

"Not all blue jays are mean," Rupert said.

"Sure they are," chirped a brown house sparrow. "Everyone knows that."

"But if one of us turned into a blue jay, we'd still play together, right?"

Spotting the lone blue jay at the feeder, the grosbeak bristled its white-speck-led, black feathers squawking, "Hey! What's that blue jay doing in our park?"

Suddenly all the birds dove, leaving Rupert behind, chasing the other blue jay away.

This troubled Rupert.

How could they be nice to him and cruel to other blue jays?

All the other birds liked Rupert, but he wanted them to like him for himself; for who he really was.

He thought of a test to find the truth.

After the blue jay was driven out of the park, the flock of birds cooled off in the bath. Rupert flapped from a branch overhanging the water and landed with a splash. His feathers returned to their brilliant shades of blue.

The grosbeak shrieked, "Blue jay!"

"You tricked us," whistled the house sparrow.

Rupert was saddened by their angry chirping and hateful glares because of how he looked. Even though they had liked Rupert and had played with him when he was in disguise, they did not accept him as he really was. He did not want to play with them anymore.

With outstretched wings, Rupert left Twin Pines beneath the angry glares of the birds.

He flew back to the cabin where he'd met Aura. Aura had not cared about how he'd looked. She'd liked the kindness inside him. The sun was warm. Rupert searched the cabin and the surrounding woods, but the caterpillar was nowhere. As the sun set, Rupert rested on the roof, feeling sad and lonely. He sighed thoughtfully. Maybe he would not find Aura and he would lose the chance for a true friend. If only I had not been so busy trying to fit in with the other birds, he thought.

"Rupert! You're back! I knew you'd be."

Rupert looked up and saw a beautiful butterfly. Its delicate wings were of so many different colors that the sight left him breathless. "Aura is that you?"

"Of course its me," Aura giggled. "I just went through a change."

"You're beautiful," Rupert whispered.

"Oh, Rupert. You're so sweet." Aura fluttered in front of Rupert. "I'm glad you came back. Come. Let's smell flowers."

Rupert smelled flowers with Aura.

He felt happier than he had ever felt before.

John P. McCarthy

was born John P. Susberry in Washington, D.C., on November 10, 1966. He says he is, "the loving creation of an interracial marriage." He changed his name to honor his grandfather, P.H. McCarthy, Jr., a pioneer lawyer during the labor movement in California. He lived in Chicago until he was 25 years old. He earned a degree in history at Illinois State University in Normal, IL, and a Master's Degree in English at State University of New York at Geneseo, where he met his wife, Kathy. The couple lives in Michigan, just north of Detroit, where he

Mr. McCarthy and his wife, Kathy

teaches English at Clarkston High School. They will be experiencing parenthood during the printing of this book with the birth of their first child in August. Other family members are their two cats, Calvin and Gen. Mr. McCarthy has had several short stories published, including *The Double-Dog Dare* in <u>WaveLength</u> (1996), *Jihad* in <u>Ultimate Writer</u> (1994), *Love's Troth* in <u>Mostly Maine</u> (1994) and an essay, *Dreams for my First Baby* in the <u>Grand Rapids Press</u> (1997). Currently, Mr. McCarthy is writing a novel about summer love and interracial relationships, based on his experiences as a teen. An additional project is the sequel to *Rupert's Gift*, tentatively titled, *Aurora's Blessing*. The themes in *Rupert's Gift* were based on John McCarthy's experiences as a young child.

Ms. Sagasti with her dog, Pretzel

Miriam Sagasti

was born in Lima, Peru. She studied interior design at the School of Interior Design and landscaping at the National Agrarian University, both in Lima, Peru. After coming to the United States, she studied graphic design, illustration and photography at N.V.C.C. in Virginia. From 1984 through 1990, Ms. Sagasti entered and placed in over twenty competitions and exhibitions all over the U.S.. She says she always wanted to illustrate children's stories, and turned her focus to doing that five years ago by sending out her work to publishers. Since then her art has been published in seven books in Barron's Education Series, in three books by publisher Kar-Ben Copies, and in two Bible Stories Books for the Mennonite Press. She has illustrated several covers and articles for both *Hopscotch Magazine for Girls* and *Boy's Quest Magazine*, she illustrated one of the *Project Take Home Books* for publisher Quarasan, has illustrated two books for the Concordia Publishing House, and seven puzzles for The Great American Puzzle Factory. Her work was selected to the 1994 International Children's Book Illustration Fair, Bologna, Italy, for the Best of International Self-Promotion Books by the Supon Design Group, and was selected for Letterhead and Logo Design 3 by Rockport Publishers. Ms. Sagasti has three grown children, all currently in graduate school. She and her husband, Leo, currently live in Chapel Hill, North Carolina.

The Perfect Shell

by Juliet L. Shepherd

*Dedicated to My Grandmother,
who appreciated the ocean's simple treasures.*

illustrated by Marie Garafano

Olivia didn't know how long her grandmother had been coming to the beach.
But she knew it had to be for a long time because she knew so much about
shells. As they walked, her grandmother pointed out the channeled whelks,
the conches, the scallops, and the moon shells.

Olivia enjoyed searching for the different kinds to add to her grandmother's collection, but she wanted to find the perfect shell. It had to be out there. She didn't know what it would look like - - what color or shape - - but she did know that when she saw it, it would strike her in a way that the others hadn't. It would carry the colors of the deepest ocean waters. It would sparkle in the sunlight. And it would feel like it belonged in her hand.

So Olivia began her search for the perfect shell. Some shells were scattered. Some were clustered in long piles that seemed to stretch forever. Some were broken, some sparkled, some seemed old, and others young. Some were buried in the sand, some were stuck in footprints.

Some were used to decorate a sandcastle - - but she didn't have the heart to take those away. Olivia even waded into the water, stretched her hands out, and caught some as they journeyed to the shore.

As she walked, Olivia wondered - - how did the shells get here? How far did they have to travel? How old were they?

Before Olivia knew it, her bag was full. She hadn't even realized that she was collecting shells as she searched. She liked so many, and wanted to add them all to her grandmother's collection.

As she emptied her bag onto the picnic table and sorted through them, she wondered if she had found the perfect shell. One looked like a trumpet. Another like a kitten's paw. One reminded her of a checkerboard, and another of a comb. One looked like it had an eye. Another like it had a bump on its head. One was a butterfly. One even had a hole in the middle. One was a prickly porcupine. Another was the same color as her Golden Retriever. Another reminded her of raspberry-swirl ice cream.

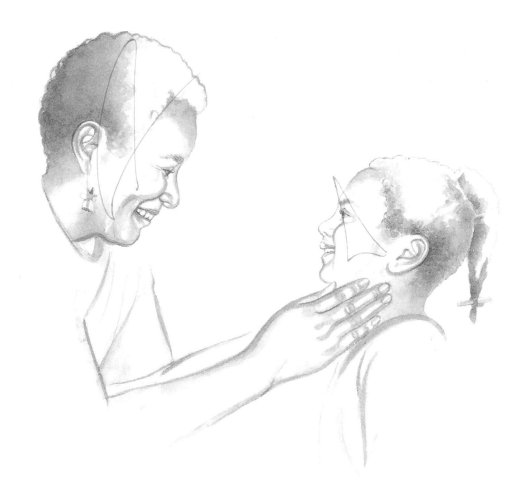

"Which one is the perfect shell?" she asked her grandmother.

Much to Olivia's surprise, her grandmother didn't even look at the pile of beautifully arrayed shells. Instead, she looked straight into Olivia's dark brown eyes.

"Olivia, my dear, there is no such thing as *the* perfect shell. They are all perfect in their own way; whether it's their shape, or color, or texture; whether they are speckled or shiny, pale baby-pink or pearly white, bumpy or curled. And I bet you won't find two that are exactly the same. Even if two look a lot alike, they are each unique. Each one traveled a different way to get here, seeing so many different things along the way. If they could talk, they'd each tell us a different story."

It wasn't until that night that Olivia understood what her grandmother meant. She had settled down for bed, taking one last look at the shells sitting on her night stand. She picked up the trumpet, the checkerboard, the porcupine.

Yes, they are all perfect, she thought.

And then she turned off the light, rested her head comfortably on her fluffy pillow, and listened to the rhythmic beating of the mysterious ocean waters - - and she wondered what other perfect shells she would find tomorrow.

Juliet Shepherd

wrote *The Perfect Shell* while vacationing in Boca Grande, Florida. Since a young girl, Ms. Shepherd has always enjoyed spending time on the beach and collecting shells. Her favorite shell collection includes the shells she gathered while writing her short story. Ms. Shepherd, an elementary school teacher, lives in Davenport, Iowa with her husband, Oliver, and their two labrador retrievers.

Marie Garafano

has been an illustrator in the Philadelphia area for the past ten years. She graduated from the Philadelphia College of Art, now part of the University of the Arts, where she studied painting and printmaking in addition to advertising design. As a freelance illustrator, Ms. Garafano enjoys the flexibility of working on a variety of projects in different media. She says "My aim is to meet her clients' needs in a way that conveys feeling, both in the emotive quality of the subject and the treatment of the line or wash."

267

Special Kids

Teddy Bears Can't Stand Up

by Noah Margo

Inspired from an original idea by Noah Margo and Joshua Margo

Dedicated to Laura Rose,
who keeps me standing.

illustrated by Erin Michelle Cardenas

Teddy Bears are colorful
Like people all around.
They come in every shade there is;
White, yellow, red or brown.

Teddy bears are brave and true
They heal with just a stitch.
And Teddy Bears can scratch your back
If you start to itch.

Teddy Bears can listen
While you're practicing to read.
And Teddy Bears don't care
If you get stuck on "TUMBLEWEED"

272

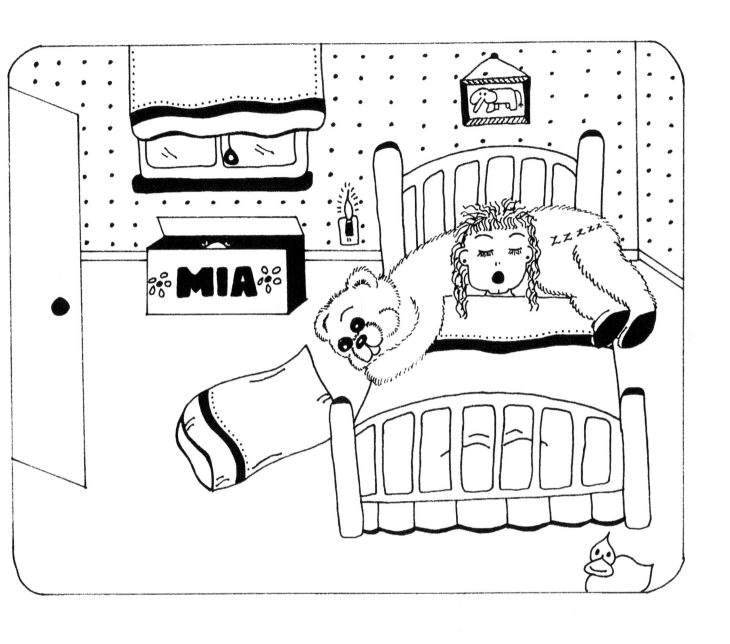

Teddy Bears can be your pillow
When yours falls off the bed.
And Teddy Bears will not wake up
while underneath your head.

Teddy Bears can keep an eye
on all your favorite things;
Like rubber balls and storybooks
and colored kites with strings.

273

Teddy Bears can take a bath
Then hang outside to dry.
Teddy Bears can be your friend
And hug you when you cry.

And Teddy Bears can star with you
in your homemade plays.
Or Teddy Bears can be your guests
for tea on Saturdays.

275

Teddy bears can fit into
All your baby clothes.
And Teddy Bears can keep you warm
When winter bites your nose.

Teddy Bears can play outside
With your dog and cat
or stay inside your closet
with your baseball, glove and bat.

Like kids who stay inside and read
While others run and play,
These children are both right you see
by having fun their way.

277

Have you ever had a Teddy Bear
that's big or one that's small?
Friends, like bears, are different too;
some are short and some are tall.

Teddy Bears are always fun
but can't do everything.
Like people who are limited
but dance while others sing.

A friend is one who stands by you
through the good and through the bad.
And even if they can't stand up
They're the best friend you ever had.

Teddy Bears can be real big
or fit inside a cup.
Teddy Bears can sit anywhere...
But Teddy Bears can't stand up.

Noah Margo

Teddy Bears. . . marks Mr. Margo's publishing debut. The author started writing after his baseball career stalled when he grounded into a triple play during the Little League championship series. Mr Margo was "born in Brooklyn, N.Y., PDM (Post-Dodgers-Move)." He has a bachelor's of arts in creative writing and literature and a master's degree in writing from the University of Southern California. While he isn't writing he says "there are loads of dirty laundry or piles of filthy dishes to attend to;" or he plays the drums with his father's 60's Doo Wopp group, The Tokens. The Tokens, if you don't remember, recorded the 1961 hit, *The Lion Sleeps Tonight*. Mr. Margo has been studying and teaching Kung Fu San Soo the past eleven years. He lives in Los Angeles with his fiance, whom he refers to as "The Amazing and Lovely" Laura Hornwood. (They exchanged nuptials during the printing of this book.) Look for their newlywed publishing debut, *People Say I'm Different*, in Cherubic Children's New Classic Storybook, Volume III.

Erin Michelle Cardenas

was born and raised in Los Angeles, California. She attended the American College for the Applied Arts where she majored in commercial art. Her talents in art range from illustration and watercolor to photography and computer graphics. She is currently a freelance artist and photographer. Her interest in illustrating children's books flourished after the birth of her son, Ethan, who was the inspiration for the look of the Teddy Bear in *Teddy Bears Can't Stand Up*. Erin and her husband, Sergio, recently had their second child, Mia. She will no doubt be the inspiration for the illustrated characters to come.

David's A.D.D.

by **Sherrill S. Cannon**

*Dedicated to David, who told me his story,
and for My Mother, Beth T. Stalker.*

illustrated by Monica Wyrick

David sometimes just couldn't sit still;
He'd fidget, and yell, and disrupt things at will;
He'd get very angry and then lose his cool.
But this didn't bother the kids in his school.

283

Whenever this happened, they'd say to each other,
"I think it is time to go call David's mother."
For whenever they found David couldn't sit still,
They thought that perhaps he'd forgotten his pill.
And Dave would go downstairs to run in the gym,
To help get out energy trapped inside him;
He'd run and he'd run, and he'd not take a break
'Til he'd swallowed the pill he'd forgotten to take.

For David had what is called A.D.D.
He couldn't see things the way others could see.
We all have a camera that lives in our head.
It gives us bright pictures of all that is said.
The lens helps us focus, to make things seem clear -
Dave's couldn't connect with his eye or his ear.
The focusing lens was asleep in his brain.
His pill helped him wake it up once again.
It helped him remember the skills that he'd learned
To help him restore self-control he had earned.

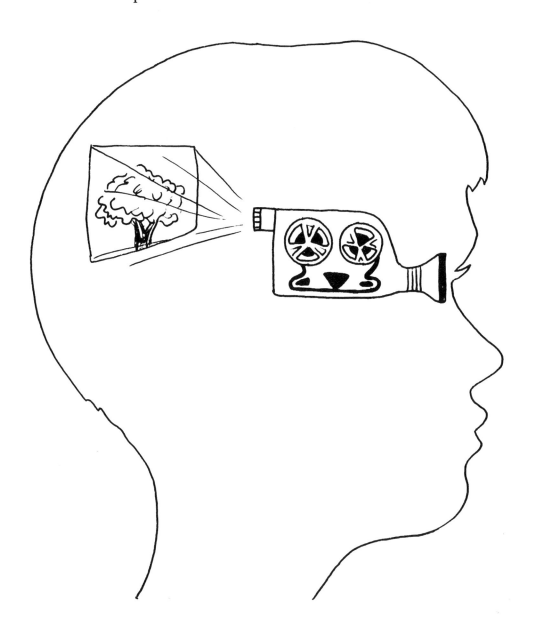

When David was young, he could not pay attention:
No matter what his mother would mention,
His mind wouldn't focus; and this made him mad -
So he'd yell and he'd scream at the problems he had.
His parents just didn't know what they should do.
He'd try to tie laces, and then throw his shoe;
He'd try to draw pictures, and then rip the page;
He seemed to be filled with a terrible rage.
He couldn't sit still, and he wouldn't obey;
"He's just hyperactive," his doctor would say.
And everyone thought he was out of control;
His violent tantrums were taking their toll.

The kids wouldn't play with him: he was too rough;
He'd push and he'd shove and he'd grab at their stuff.
Nobody liked him or wanted him near;
And he seemed to be getting worse, year after year.

287

Finally his father said, "This has to stop!
David's our son and we love him a lot.
I really don't care about what others say,
There must a reason he's acting this way."

After some testing, the doctors found out
That David had what they were learning about:
That some children lacked a certain dimension.
A.D.D. meant they could not pay attention.
"Attention Deficit Disorder", they said,
A small lazy link somewhere in the head;
A sleepy connection that wasn't so good.
It didn't use sugar the way that it should.
But now there was hope, there was new medicine;
And ways they'd discovered to help kids fit in:
The pills might awaken that small sleepy link,
Allowing these children to be able to think:
To concentrate on what they needed to know;
To learn how to read, and to learn how to grow.
To learn the best way to fit into a group,
No longer to have to be out of the loop.
Some might need medicine, others would not;
Most could improve with new ways being taught.

For this was not all David would have to do;
He'd have to adjust, and his parents would too.
He'd follow a schedule his parents would set:
A step-by-step list so he wouldn't forget
What time to get up, and get dressed, make his bed,
And clean up his room, as his parents had said,
What time to have breakfast, get ready for school.
It seemed to be helpful to follow a rule.

And if he could manage to do things on time,
He'd go to the grab-bag to see what he'd find:
His grab-bag was filled with erasers and gum
And other surprises as prizes he'd won.

291

His teachers at school showed him ways he could cope;
They helped him to learn and they offered him hope.
He found a computer would help him to write;
He could think faster as he learned to type;
He'd get his thoughts out, and he'd feel so much better
When he didn't struggle with forming each letter.

He'd have to do homework, and schedule each class:
Ten minutes for science, and fifteen for math,
Ten more for spelling; and if all were all right,
He'd get extra time to watch TV that night.
The ground rules were set for each thing overall;
For trips to the movies and trips to the mall:
No running, no screaming, no wandering away;
He'd have to behave if he wanted to stay.
If he lost control when they all went to town,
He'd stay in the car until he could calm down.
But if he were good, he would get a reward - -
Perhaps with a stop at the video store!

So Dave took his medicine day after day;
He learned how to work, and he learned how to play.
He learned to make friends, for he learned to behave;
To listen to teachers, instructions they gave.
He learned to communicate, share what he thought.
He read lots of books, and he used what they taught:
He learned origami that's done in Japan,
(And proved he'd extended his attention span!).
He made little flowers and birds out of paper,
And made a small frog which he gave to a neighbor.
He liked to craft things, like his gumball machine
With a handle that turned a base painted green.
And David was proud of the things he could do -
He knew he was smart, and was glad that he knew!
David could share special gifts that he had:
He'd make his mom smile, and he'd calm down for his dad!

Now Dave's controlling the way that he acts;
He knows what he has, understands all the facts.
He takes medication to help him to live
A life where he's happy and has gifts to give.
He never stops trying to master the skill
Of paying attention or just sitting still.

He copes with his A.D.D. day after day,
He knows it may possibly not go away;
But he's learned to accept it, and go on to be
A symbol of hope for those with A.D.D.

294

Sherrill S. Cannon

is a magna cum laude graduate of the American University, and has been writing lyrical poetry since her seventh grade "Poetry Club" at National Cathedral School in Washington D.C. Some of her poetry has already been published in various collections. In addition to a ten-year teaching career in Washington, D.C., she was also a journalist and photographer in the Northern Virginia area. Following a move to the Philadelphia area, she became a stage-manager and light/sound technician for Peddler's Village Dinner Theatre, as well as an assistant to Cathy Parker Talent Management (for whom she wrote a *Handbook* which is in its third edition.) She is now a computer consultant and office manager in Binghamton, N.Y. Married to her husband Kim for 37 years, she is a mother of four (K.C., Kell, Kerry and Cailin) and grandmother of four (Josh, Parker, Colby and Lindsay.) She has also written three musical plays for elementary school children (K-3) and each has been produced to critical acclaim. The daughter of an elementary school teacher, she is also the mother of an elementary school teacher. Another of her stories is currently under contract with a literary agent. *David's A.D.D.* was written in response to a friend's son, who liked her stories and wished there were a story for "kids like me." Now there is!

Monica Wyrick

Self-portrait by the artist

has had many years of experience in the art world. She spent five yeara as art director at an advertising agency in Ohio and then three years as the in-house art director at a large hospital in Georgia. She says that since the birth of her first child eight years ago, she has been doing freelance illlustration for various agencies and individuals. The past three years she has turned her focus toward children's art and portraits. The artist says, "My goal is to break into the children's book market." Ms. Wyrick is an accomplished artist in a number of mediums and illustration styles. She has also written and illustrated a children's book that is being considered for publication at several publishing houses. During the time this book was being printed, Ms. Wyrick and her family moved from Olney, Maryland to Apex, North Carolina.

My Brother has a Brain Injury

by **Alvin Robert Cunningham**

*Dedicated to the Memory of
My Loving Mother,
Lorene Cunningham*

illustrated by **Brian Kammerer**

My older brother and I are great pals.

We like to ride our bikes together. He likes to ride his bicycle very fast.

One day he fell off and hit his head.

An ambulance took him to the hospital.

When he woke up, my parents and I were very happy.

The doctors taught him how to walk and talk again.

When he left the hospital, we had a "Welcome Home" party.

That summer, I helped him with his exercises

And I listened to him read.

When school started, he was in a special class. The doctors said that his brain was injured and his special teachers would help him learn.

Some of his friends thought that he walked and talked funny. But Mom and Dad said that he was very brave.

Now, we wear bicycle helmets when we ride.

My older brother and I will always be great pals.

This story is endorsed by the National Brain Injury Association in Washington, D.C.

The Brain Injury Association provides information on how to prevent these complicated, difficult disabilities. Nationally every year about 25,000 traumatic brain injuries are received by children on bicycles. The Brain Injury Association's national preventive education program of "Head Smart" helps to teach school age children the importance of wearing helmets while bicycling. *Research shows that helmet use while bicycling can reduce the chance of sustaining a brain injury by almost 90%.* The Association also informs parents, teachers and other adults what devastating permanent injuries can and do occur without helmets, and how the results of brain injury by children affects home and school life.

<u>The National Office of the Brain Injury Association is located at:</u>

1776 Massachusetts Avenue, NW, Suite #100
Washington, D.C. 20036

Phone number: (202) 296-6443

Alvin Robert Cunningham

has been an elementary teacher for the past 27 years and is a traumatic brain injury survivor of a 1989, one-car, automobile accident. Like the brother in this story, the author was in a coma for three weeks and in a major trauma hospital for two months. Mr. Cunningham was left with permanent physical and neurological impairment. He has learned to cope with this disability and hasn't missed a day of work since his return in May, 1990. Being a full-time, brain-injured teacher, he has become a model and a source of inspiration to the brain injured/special education students in his district. Mr. Cunningham is currently a Contributing Editor to the Christian publication *Head to Head*, The Magazine for Brain Injury Survivors (St. Johnbury, VT). He is also the published author of the middle reader novel *United We Stand* , (Aegina Press/University Editions 1991, Huntington, WV) and *Our Principal is a Werewolf*, Kabel Publishers, 1996 (Rockville, MD), a collection of humorous, school poems.

Brian Kammerer

has been a resident of New Caanan, Connecticut for the past ten years although he works in New York City. He is an established commercial illustrator and has worked on many national and worldwide advertising campaigns for such clients as Coca-Cola, Camel, Milton Bradley, Sharp and Bristol-Myers. Mr. Kammerer holds degrees in Film, Art and History from Denison University in Granville, Ohio. He will often combine his love and interest in American history to create his artwork. The result has been a series of painting, drawings and dioramas on the Civil War. He is currently completing a 5' by 20' mural of Pickett's Charge which he hopes to have displayed by the National Park in Gettysburg, Pennsylvania in the future. Mr. Kammerer's artwork has been exhibited at the American Folk Art Museum and Cartiers in New York City, the International Maritime Exhibit at Mystic Seaport Museum and the Women's Club in Bronxville, New York. Mr. Kammerer has also published a series of lithographs depicting children and the ocean entitled *The Winged Fantasy Collection*. His work is now found in both corporate and private collections.

Wisdom

Emily Said

by Stacey Allison Taylor

*Dedicated to My Husband, Bruce,
and My Children,
Sarah, Jake and Hudson*

illustrated by Sheryl Koby

Emily said that I am her best friend and that we always have to sit next to each other at snack time.

Emily said that she has to go first whenever we play a game because she is taller than me.

Emily said that if you get lipstick on your skin you have to wipe it off with your fingers or you'll get a rash.

When I showed Emily a boo-boo on my leg she said it was something called a pimple and when her big sister gets them she squeezes them until they pop.

Once, when I was eating an apple, Emily said that if I eat the apple seed I will grow an apple tree in my tummy.

I went to Emily's house to play and she has lots of great toys. I asked her if I could play with one of her dolls that had on a pink dress, but Emily said that today was Tuesday and that doll had to sleep all day on Tuesday so I could not play with her.

Emily and I got hungry at her house so she made us tuna fish with peanut
butter and ketchup. It was pretty messy but Emily said that she eats this all
the time and that I had to finish mine all up because it makes you grow.

Emily said that when she grows up she's going to be an acrobat in the circus
and she'll wear a bright pink costume with sparkles and feathers
on it.

One time, when we were at school, Emily said that we had to trade cookies because hers was round with green sprinkles on it and mine was a star with red sprinkles and that red was her favorite color. I looked at my cookie and I looked at her cookie and then I said, "NO!"

I don't even think I believe everything that Emily said.

Stacey Allison Taylor

moved from Slate Hill, New York, to St. Peters, Missouri, this past spring, with her husband, Bruce, and three children, Sarah, Jake and Hudson. Ms. Taylor graduated from Thomas Edison State College with a BA in Business Administration. She says, "Currently I am a full-time, stay-at-home mom." *Emily Said* is her first published work. Another story she wrote, *Who Broke the Moon?* is currently being considered for publication. The author says, "My children are a never-ending source of interesting ideas for children's stories." When asked about the creation of *Emily Said*, the author remarked, "My six year old daughter has a friend who is always entertaining us with her stories and ideas. A few of these were written down to form *Emily Said*." The author added, "I think it is important for children to learn that they don't always have to believe everything someone says; especially a friend with an overactive imagination." Ms. Taylor says she wants children to learn to think for themselves and not to be afraid to say "No!" This story is to help them toward that goal.

Sheryl Koby

is a free-lance artist concentrating on portraits, wall murals and illustrating children's stories. Ms. Koby works with pencils, pastels, acrylics, pen and ink. She attended Kent State University for Art. Last year Ms. Koby illustrated one story in our Cherubic Children's New Classic Story Book, Volume One. This year she has illustrated two stories for us in Volume Two. Ms. Koby resides in Rockledge, Florida with her husband, Tom, and their four growing children (Paul, Drew, Emily, & Cory along with their newest family member, Ezra, the entertaining Lilac Siamese.

Where Does the Time Go?

by Scott and Jennifer Arney

*Dedicated to those who know the importance
and priceless value of time spent with loved ones.*

illustrated by John Clarke

At first it seems that time goes so slowly,
As slowly as the clock ticks,
As slowly as a lollipop licks,
Time goes slowly.

Especially in the winter season,
And for no particular reason,
You don't even feel like teasin',
Your sister, your brother,
Not even your mother.
Time goes slowly.

Time never goes slower than when you are in school.
When you are forced to obey all the rules.
You read and study and write,
Sometimes even at night.

But then, you put away your science kit,
And wonder if your swimsuit fits.
And you think for a minute,
School's not out for the summer yet, is it?
Does time go slowly?

It's time for some ice cream!
Can this be a dream?
Are those fireworks that I hear?
Can it be that time of year?
Does time not go so slowly?

Time for school again?
I remember when,
I could stay outside and play,
Every single day.
Is the future far away?

Why are the leaves turning pretty colors?
Why are people closing their shutters?
Where did summer go?
Is it fall and I didn't know?
Just where did that time go?

Winter comes and goes.
The spring winds blow and blow!
Summer's back and then it's not;
Now it's time for the turkey trot!

At first it seems so hard to believe,
Does time have a trick up its sleeve?
Why does time seem to go slowly and then fast?
Why don't the things that happened in the past, last?

The truth be told, is worth more than gold;
Time always goes the same speed!
It may seem to go slowly, it may seem to go fast,
But it really just follows your lead.

So, don't worry or wonder too much,
About where time goes and such.
Just take time to do the things you like,
Like riding your bike or flying a kite!

Scott Arney & Jennifer Arney

were both born and raised in the Chicago, Illinois area. They are married and currently reside in Naperville, Illinois. Ms. Arney is an aspiring artist and comic strip creator. Mr. Arney says that he is "an international man of mystery, who has been inspired by his wife to express his creativity." The couple write and create stories largely because they enjoy sharing them with their six nieces and nephews and two younger sisters. Although this is their first published story, they are in the process of attempting to publish many more. The couple reports that, in reference to their being published in Cherubic Children's New Classic Story Book, Volume Two, they are "thrilled to be a part of this special project." We are thrilled to have their first published story as part of our collection.

Self-portrait by the artist

John Clarke

graduated from the Art Institute of Boston as an Illustration Major in May, 1991. Some of his clients include The Boston Phoenix, IBM, The Chicago Tribune, Webmaster Magazine, and The Boston Red Sox. He currently resides in Brighton, Massachusetts with two small frogs.

The Cloud that Covered My Head

by Ilana K. Levinsky

Dedicated to
My Daughter, Maya.

illustrated by Shauna M. Kawasaki

I never liked to wake up in the morning and go to school, because when I was asleep I would do a lot of exciting things. I would be riding my bicycle, swinging high on the swing or maybe eating some chocolate ice cream.

Mom would force me out of bed and I would say, wait a minute, let me have just one more bite of ice cream or stay another minute on the swing or something. Mom would tell me that I had just been dreaming and that nothing that I did or ate in a dream was real and to please get up and go to school.

In school I sat at my desk staring at the sun outside the room. I thought to myself that dreaming was much more fun then anything else that I have done, certainly more fun than school because in my dreams I could do whatever I wished.

One morning as I was sitting at my desk, I stared through the window as I usually did and then it happened all over again. I started to see all those wonderful things that only appeared in my dreams. I was going on the rides in an amusement park and nobody told me when to stop and how much cotton candy to eat. I was also playing ball and scoring all the goals in the field. I also went to a great big toy store and got all the toys I would normally have to wait for and only get on a holiday or birthday. Then suddenly I heard the school bell ring which meant that school was over and it was time to go home again.

I became really good at this daydreaming thing and didn't mind so much getting up in the morning anymore because I knew that more dreams were waiting for me in school.

One morning when I woke up Mom told me that I had a cloud around my head, and that it must be because my head is in the clouds most of the time with all those dreams of mine. I thought that a cloud around my head was great. My dreams also became more exciting and a little bit strange. I was flying airplanes and sailing ships. I was sometimes fighting dragons and at other times acting like a princess. I saw elephants with wings and dogs that could talk.

I was daydreaming now all the time. I couldn't tell which was day and which was night, nor what was a dream and what was not.

Once when I was daydreaming in school, as I usually did, the bell rang and instead of going home like the rest of the kids, I just stayed in my seat continuing my dream. The janitor in school woke me up and told me to hurry up and go home, otherwise my mom would be very worried about my whereabouts.

I stared at the janitor with a puzzled look because I couldn't remember where I actually lived- - whether on the clouds or in the jungle in Africa, or was it in the igloo I just saw?

Luckily my mom happened to walk right into class. She hugged me and said that she thought that I was late because that cloud around my head was engaging me in another dream.

The cloud around my head became really thick and it was getting hard to see, smell and eat. Also, it wasn't very comfortable to be rained on from the neck down.

I thought that maybe dreaming should remain for the night, because at day-time there were other things which I sort of missed.

333

The next night I went to sleep and had another nice dream, but in the morning I said good-bye. It's time to get up to go to school. You wait here in bed, and I'll come back really soon.

From then on I always left my dreams in bed.

Ilana Karen Levinsky

was born in London, England, in 1966. She spent her childhood years in Israel. She served in the Israeli Army in Intelligence. Following that, she studied law at the University of Manchester, England. She now resides in Scottsdale, Arizona, together with her daughter, Maya. The Cloud that Covered My Head is her first published story which was inspired by her daughter. She has also written television scripts.

Shauna Mooney Kawasaki

was born in Provo, Utah , October 20, 1953. She has three sisters and two brothers. The author says, "I was born with a pencil in one hand, a pen in the other, and a paint brush behind my ear. Ms. Kawasaki says she barely made it through high school. She taught herself to draw, illustrate, sew, carve, and make toys. She got a job in advertising, about which she commented, "I worked in that stinky business until 1977." She was hired as an art director for a children's magazine in 1990. The author states, "after living as a very happy and content old-maid aunty, to my boss, a wonderful widower with 7 wonderful children, I married the boss - - not a good career move! So now I am a free lance illustrator, toymaker, mother with lots of bills." Ms. Kawasaki has illustrated five books that she wrote, and has illustrated many others. She told us that she does not like cats, but loves "reading, monsters, sewing, robots, drawing, traveling, vintage sports cars, teasing anyone around me and eating."

PENELOPE AND HER INVISIBLE POOCH

by **Carolyn Yencharis**

*Dedicated to My Parents,
Beverly and Ralph Johnston,
and Traci and Jen.*

illustrated by Sheryl Koby

Penelope's tenth birthday was coming in one month, and she wanted a dog.
But her parents objected.

"A dog is a lot of responsibility, honey. Between school, homework and your household chores, how will you find the time to take care of it? Dogs need a lot of attention, and besides they cost money."

"But I will be responsible," protested Penelope. "I promise I'll walk it every day and feed it and - - oh pleeeeassse. . ." Penelope flashed the toothiest smile and droopiest eyes she could muster, her 'irresistible look' she liked to call it.

"No," said her parents sternly. "How do we know that a ten year old girl can handle such a big responsibility?"

Penelope felt her face turn to a pout but stopped it quickly. "My parents are right. I need to show them that I can take care of a dog. Hmmm." Penelope thought hard about it. Finally, Penelope's face lit up. She had an idea.

The next morning Penelope woke up early. "Good morning," she said to her parents, and she walked downstairs to the basement. She opened the door. "Good morning, Zooey. How are you today? Are you ready for your walk? Yes, yes, yes, that's a good poochy. C'mon." Penelope grabbed a rope from the floor and made a loop at one end. She held it like a leash and took it upstairs.

Her parents looked perplexed. "Who's Zooey, honey?"

"This is," she said pointing to the loop. "I'm taking her for a walk."

Ten minutes later Penelope came back, took the loop down to the basement and brought it a bowl of water and some meat loaf from last night's dinner.

"I have to get ready for school, Zooey, but I'll be home at two thirty. Bye." She kissed Zooey on her invisible forehead.

During the next three weeks Penelope walked her invisible pooch three times a day. She played with Zooey in between taking out the garbage and cleaning her room. She taught Zooey to roll over and sit. She invited Zooey up to her room while she did her homework. She bought dog food and a dog bed with money she had saved from past birthdays. And she even called the local doggy obedience schools to see if Zooey could enroll. She lavished love and attention on Zooey every day, and she made sure to never allow Zooey on Mom's good furniture.

But one day, Penelope woke up sick. "Oh, honey," said her father. "How is your fever? Do you want me to take Zooey outside for you?" He had really come to love the invisible dog.

"No, Dad, I have it covered," she assured him.

Ten minutes later Penelope's best friend Charlie was knocking at the front door to come and take Zooey for a walk; Charlie had come to love Zooey too.

Penelope recovered from the flu just in time for her tenth birthday. She woke up and jumped out of bed; she felt great! "I can't wait to see Zooey!" she said to her reflection in the mirror. She walked downstairs.

"Good morning and happy birthday!" her parents called, flashing huge smiles across their faces.

"Good morning and thank you!" Penelope smiled and headed toward the basement with her rope-leash.

"WOOF. . . WOOF. . ." she heard at the basement door. Wow, I'm even starting to hear invisible barks, she thought to herself.

Penelope opened the door, and sitting in front of her, wagging its tail was a real dog! "Oh Zooey, you're just like I imagined you to be," she exclaimed as she hugged the dog.

"Here's another birthday present, honey." Her mother handed her a red dog leash.

"Thanks Mom and Dad." Penelope smiled and gave her parents the biggest hug she had ever given.

Carolyn Yencharis

graduated from Susquehanna University in 1993. She studied English Literature and Economics and was a recipient of the Charles A. Rahter scholarship for outstanding English majors. Ms. Yencharis currently resides in Tokyo, Japan where she is the head foreign instructor at the Tokyo Pacific Business College. When not teaching, the author enjoys traveling in Asian countries such as Thailand, India and Nepal. She began writing children's stories two and a half years ago upon her arrival in Japan. This is the first time she is being published.

Sheryl Koby

is a free-lance artist concentrating on portraits, wall murals and illustrating children's stories. Ms. Koby works with pencils, pastels, acrylics, pen and ink. She attended Kent State University for Art. Last year Ms. Koby illustrated one story, *Lucy and the Rainy Day*, for *Cherubic Children's New Classic Story Book, Volume One*, her first foray into illustrating children's stories. This year she has illustrated two stories in this story book (Volume Two). She resides in Rockledge, Florida, with her husband, Tom, and their four young children.

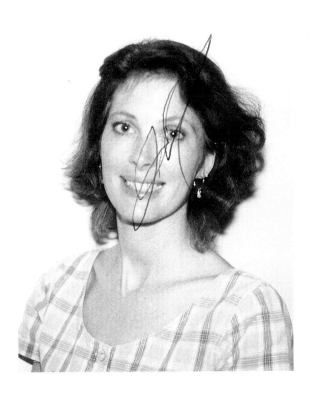

Jacob's Job

by Diane Howell

*Dedicated to
Brendan*

illustrated by Maury Ann Brooks

Jacob has a job.

He earns one penny per piece, providing he makes good choices. Each bad choice costs him two pennies.

Jacob picks apples.

Every day after school he rushes home, has a quick snack, and changes into work clothes. If all goes well he makes it to Farmer Fiddle's by half past four, giving him one full hour of picking time.

Jacob had been picking apples since September. By his last count he needed only two more weeks to save enough pennies to reach his goal.

One Wednesday Jacob was delayed at school. Even though he skipped his snack he arrived half an hour late for work.

In a panic, Jacob began picking at a feverish pace. To his relief he still managed to fill his basket despite the late start.

Farmer Fiddle counted carefully as he emptied Jacob's harvest.

"Well, Jacob. I see you have thirty fine red apples in your basket today. That would normally earn you thirty pennies. But look," he paused.

Jacob's face reddened as he noticed the five rotten apples. Reluctantly he returned ten cents to Farmer Fiddle.

"I'll try harder tomorrow" he promised.

That night at dinner Jacob's Mom and Dad sensed that something was troubling him. When they learned he had to return ten cents to Farmer Fiddle, they gently reminded him of the importance of doing a careful job.

"I'll try harder tomorrow," Jacob assured them.

The next day Jacob arrived at Farmer Fiddle's fifteen minutes early. As he removed each apple from the tree he carefully rolled it in his hand, inspecting for even the tiniest spot or bump. Any apple that was not *perfect* was placed directly in the pig trough.

At the end of the day Farmer Fiddle quietly set about his counting.

"Not quite so many apples today, Jacob" he said slowly. Jacob hung his head. "No sir."

"But," Farmer Fiddle smiled, "these are the best choices you've ever made!"

When Jacob burst into his house that night he could hardly wait to tell his Mom and Dad the news.

For his careful work he had earned twenty-five cents *plus* a bonus of one nickel! Now, by his calculation, he only needed to earn sixty-three more pennies to reach his goal.

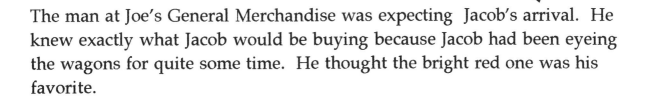

Jacob continued to work slowly and carefully each day and soon managed to earn the money he needed. He spent an entire Saturday counting and rolling his pennies until finally he was ready.

The man at Joe's General Merchandise was expecting Jacob's arrival. He knew exactly what Jacob would be buying because Jacob had been eyeing the wagons for quite some time. He thought the bright red one was his favorite.

Jacob likes to call his new wagon an "apple cart." Not just because it's shiny and red, or because he now uses it for hauling apples. He calls it an "apple cart" because it seems as if he picked a *million* apples to earn it!

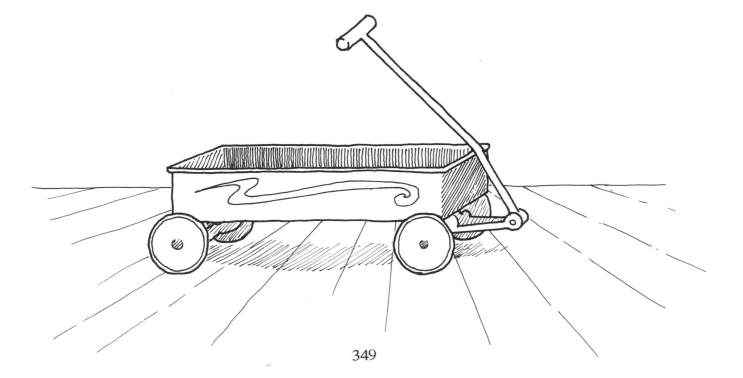

Jacob still goes to work every day.

He hopes to keep his job for a very long time because by his estimation he will need to pick another *trillion* apples to earn what he wants next - an apple bike!

Diane Howell

was born and educated in Canada. The author says that her story, Jacob's Job, was inspired as she was watching her young son's dedication to learning new tasks. After living for a period in Alaska, Ms. Howell has now returned to her home town of Calgary, where she lives with her husband and two sons.

Maury Ann Brooks

a professional artist, Ms. Brooks runs her own arts production company, Wind Pudding Productions. She studied art at Kutztown State College and after receiving a Masters Degree in painting from Hunter College in New York, she decided to pursue her interest in children's books. Making a dramatic change from large format abstract paintings, she now works with watercolor, and pen and ink on a much smaller scale. Ms. Brooks has also developed an interest in puppetry, carving several marionettes and constructing small sets using wood, wire, fabric, discarded detergent bottles, paper mache and old canvases for backdrops. She is currently working on a picture book featuring three of these puppets. Ms. Brooks has traveled in Europe, North Africa, Turkey and Alaska, and has lived in Paris for two years. She has a strong interest in nature and loves to read. Ms. Brooks lives and works in New York with her husband, a teacher.

The People of Grey

by **Jan Fellerman**

Dedicated to my sons, Joshua and Zachary,
who should experience the joys of color,
yet be colorblind.

illustrated by Lee Green

There once was a town called Grey,
where life was the same, day after day.

The people of Grey looked like each other,
whether Mom, Dad, Sister, or Brother.
From the hair on their heads to the shoes that they wore,
the people of Grey were always a bore.

There was no laughter, joy or fun.
No one smiled, not anyone.

Each morning at seven they all would rise,
eat the same breakfast and say their goodbyes.
To school or work they left at eight,
and were home at six so not to be late.

Even their houses, in long tidy rows,
looked just alike. And on it goes.

It seemed so dull in the town of Grey.
Day after day, it was always that way.
Their clothes all the same without color or pattern.
Being the same, it would seem, was all that mattered.

As so it was, and so it would be,
that life in this town was quite ordinary.

Until one day when out of the blue,
the people of Grey met the people of Hue.
For the Hues came to visit and decided to stay,
bringing their families from far, far away.

Who were these strangers that moved into town?
The Greys were upset, with their lives turned around.

The Hues were so different, a colorful clan.
From red and orange to purple and tan.
They didn't look like the Greys
or share the same ways.
Some wore sweaters and others wore coats.
Some liked biscuits and others liked toast.

Take the Greens, for example, a family of four.
With big brother Jake and little Lenore.
Each one looked different, each one unique.
There was nothing about them in any way bleak.

They settled in Grey and Jake started school.
What he didn't expect was something quite cruel.
For the students from Grey teased the student from Hue
because of his color. Jake felt so blue.

Yet after a while the kids realized
that Jake was the same - - on the inside.
He was smart and funny and gentle and kind.
He loved to play games and he laughed all the time.

While the children began to see beyond color,
their parents still couldn't accept one another.

It was simply too much for the Greys to bear.
The Hues' arrival was a terrible scare!
But just when the Greys said enough was enough,
they began to see some incredible stuff.

Their children wore colors and styled their hair.
In bold prints and patterns, their parents did stare!

The children were happy, smiling and cheery.
The town was so vibrant, and no longer dreary.
The Hues brought laughter, joy and fun
to all the Greys, to everyone.

And that was when the Greys discovered
that people are people, no matter their color.

Jan Fellerman

is a full-time mother of two boys, ages four and six. When she is not chauffeuring Joshua or chasing Zachary, Jan enjoys golfing, traveling and writing. She recently began writing children's stories as a way to educate her sons about important social issues. *The People of Grey* was inspired by a desire to teach the meaning of tolerance in a "kid-friendly" manner. The author says, "In my prior life, I attended the University of California at Santa Cruz, Hebrew University in Jerusalem, Israel (Education Abroad Program), and Pepperdine University School of Law in Malibu, California." Although she is an attorney, Ms. Fellerman chose a career in public relations and advertising, a field, she says, she will resume when her children are older. Ms. Fellerman and her husband of 12 years, Ian, reside east of San Francisco, in Walnut Creek, California.

Lee Green

states that she has been drawing and painting since "before I can remember." She says she likes to think of herself as "untrainable;" that is, she continues, "I prefer living in blissful ignorance of the rules rather than knowingly break them." Ms. Green says that for the illustrations in this story, and many other of her works, she uses no references, but likes to "start right on the composition and see what happens." She is currently working on an illustrated edition of stories in prose and verse. She is also active in community theatre, and enjoys designing and painting stage sets. Ms. Green lives and works in Buffalo, New York.

Wind Spirit

by Lois Kipnis and John F. DeCarlo

Dedicated to Joan Bloomgarden.
Thanks for the creative connection.

illustrated by Louise Goldenberg

The Wind Spirit looked down on earth.

He saw a young boy alone, abandoned along the shore, a starfish near his feet.

He looked again. Miles away, on the shore of a seaside village, he saw an old man, alone.

He paused. He gathered his force. He began to swirl around the boy and the starfish began to glow.

In the village, the leaves on the trees were still, but the wind was howling. Dogs were barking and people were frightened. They could not feel the wind, or see any sign of a storm. All they heard was the sound of the wind howling.

As the young boy was being blown around by the wind, the starfish sparkled and circled around him. He caught it. The wind stopped and dropped him on the edge of the village.

No one saw him land. They just looked up and saw a young boy walking by, clutching a starfish in his hand.

He smiled at them. Afraid, they did not return his greetings. Every one remained still as he passed by. No one knew where he came from, or why he was there. They only knew that the sound of the wind was gone.

He did not hear their frightened whispers as they disappeared into the safety of their homes.

Not knowing where to go, and not understanding why all doors were shut to him, he followed the salty smell of the sea and sat along the seashore, holding his starfish for comfort.

As he listened to the waves splash against the shore, he heard a song. It seemed to come from a large rock near the shore. As he listened, he was lulled to sleep. There he lay in he dark of the night, a mound of sand for a pillow and his gently glowing starfish at his side.

The gulls flapping their wings woke him in the morning. The sea sparkled, and his starfish seemed silver in the morning light. Thinking of the song he had heard, he wiped the sand from his eyes and picked up his starfish.

He walked to the village. A group of children were playing. "Good morning!" the boy said, smiling his friendly grin. The children ignored him and continued to play. He thought perhaps they didn't hear him. "Hello!" he said again, still smiling. "Would any of you like to see my starfish? It shines! Sometimes it's silver. Sometimes it's gold!"

"Yeah, right!" said one child.

Another child laughed, "You are just like that crazy old man who lives by the edge of the sea." Everyone laughed at that.

One of the children grabbed the starfish and began tossing it back and forth, teasing him about his "stupid shining starfish."

Another child skipped over to the group. "Hey remember, our parents told us not to play with him. Let's go somewhere else to play."

As they ran off, he heard the echoes of their laughter. He picked up his star-fish and walked on. There was a man whittling wood. "Hey, Mister, would you like to see my starfish?"

"Boy, I don't know who you are, or what you're doing here, but scat! I've got work to do. Can't be bothered with your stupid starfish."

And so, he went from person to person. Everyone thought him weird, strange, crazy. They cast him out of the village. With a new sense of sadness on his face, he walked slowly away with the starfish in his hand.

As he wondered, "Where do I go from here?" a gentle breeze caressed his face. Again he heard a song coming from the edge of the sea near a rock. He fol-lowed the sound. He stopped. He looked, and near the big rock was an old man preparing his boat and singing a song:

> "The wind blows.
> Where it leads,
> No one knows.
>
> The wind controls
> The tide, the sea,
> A shining starfish;
> You and me.
>
> Close your eyes,
> Trust its spirit.
> It always guides.
> Never fear it."

The boy cautiously approached the man. He was about to speak, when the old man looked up and said, "What's that in your hand?"

Their eyes met, and the boy's eyes lit up with excitement. "Oh, that's my starfish. It shines!"

The old man inquired, "Where did you find it?"

The boy hesitated, "If I told you how I got it, you'd probably laugh at me."

"Oh no," the old man replied. "I'd never laugh at you. Would you like to go out to sea with me and share you story?"

"Can I? I'd love to!"

As the old man helped the boy into the boat, he carefully placed his starfish on the shore.

The old man hurried him on. "Push us out a bit, son, and hop in. Since there's no night light in the sky, we need to be back before dark."

Eager to set sail, the boy pushed the boat out on the water and climbed in, leaving his starfish behind.

Meanwhile, the same group of children who had teased the boy were fishing from a nearby rock. They noticed the boy and the old man sailing off to sea. "Hey, there go those two crazy fools!"

As another boy ran to the shore to look, he noticed the starfish. "Look, there's his starfish. Let's go get it."

They picked it up and tossed it back and forth laughing and ridiculing the boy and the old man.

"Hey, said one of them. "Let's see who can throw it the farthest!"

One boy boasted about having the strongest arm, and took it, flinging it as far as he could. It shattered against a rock into hundreds of little pieces. Suddenly the wind howled. The sand on the beach began to swirl around the children. They screamed, but their cries were drowned out by the howling wind. They raised their arms up to protect their eyes, but the wind and the crashing waves knocked them to the ground.

Suddenly the wind swept the shattered pieces of the starfish up into the sky. Like a fast moving rocket, they swirled out of sight.

As the waves pulled the children out to sea, the old man and the boy heard their cries. The boy rowed with all his might, struggling against the waves.

The boy noticed a rope on the boat and tossed it with all his might to the children.

The children caught hold of the rope, and the boy and old man towed them to the safety of the secluded cove.

As the boy stepped out of the boat, he noticed a tiny piece of his starfish. He reached down and gently picked it up. Broken hearted, he wondered if he ever would find the rest of the pieces. A teardrop rolled from the corner of his eye.

But something else caught his attention. The wind had stopped. All was perfectly still.

Relieved, the children thanked the old man and the boy. Together, they all made their way back to the village.

The boy held tightly to the broken piece of starfish in his hand.

Returning to the cave later that night, the boy told the old man that he was sad that his special starfish was lost.

The old man comforted him. "Don't worry, tomorrow we'll go out to sea again. Maybe we'll find a new starfish. In the meantime, rest." And the old man lulled him to sleep with his song:

"The wind blows.
Where it leads,
No one knows.

The wind controls
The tide, the sea,
A shining starfish;
You and me.

Close your eyes,
Trust its spirit.
It always guides.
Never fear it."

Glad to be home, the children explained to their parents all that had occurred. Moved by their story, the parents vowed to thank the old man and the boy in the morning.

As the village slept that night, the children, still shaken from their experience, could not sleep. They kept hearing the distant sound of howling wind circling around them. Curious, each one peeked out his window and beheld the strangest sight! Small stars, like miniature starfish, were gently being placed in the sky. It almost seemed as if an invisible hand was carefully placing them there.

At the same time, a few miles away, the boy looked down at the piece of star-fish in the palm of his hand and noticed it was glowing again! He then looked up into the sky and beheld the same wondrous sight. He smiled, knowing that the rest of the starfish was safe.

371

The next morning the parents and the children went down to the sea to thank the boy and the old man, and to invite them to come live in the village, but it seemed as if they were gone.

However, the boy who had shattered the starfish against the rock noticed the sail of their boat out to sea. "There goes the old man and the boy," he said. "I wish they had stayed long enough for me to apologize and show my appreciation to them." Everyone felt the same way.

The villagers watched the boat fade out of sight.

Sensing they would never see the old man and the boy again, they hoped and prayed that wherever the old man and the boy settled, their kindness to the village would be repaid. They knew in their hearts that for the rest of their lives, whenever they looked up at the stars in the sky, they would remember the boy and the old man.

The Wind Spirit looked down at the villagers. He was pleased with their newborn respect.

He looked down at the boy and the old man out at sea, together.

He felt content.

Lois Kipnis &
John DeCarlo

Ms. Kipnis is a drama specialist, educator, and author who holds a BFA from Boston University. She develops and implements "hands-on" drama workshops for students and teachers, and is a presenter at conferences for theatre, reading, arts in education, and Whole Language. She co-authored *Have You Ever, Bringing Literature to Life through Creative Dramatics*, and *The Royal Rhymer's Timer*.

John DeCarlo and Lois Kipnis

Mr. DeCarlo earned a BA from Brandeis University and a M. Div. from Union Theological Seminary. He currently teaches English at Hofstra University, where he is also pursuing a degree in Elementary Education. An actor/director, he is currently traveling as a storyteller, and has co-authored *The Royal Rhymer's Timer*.

Louise Goldenberg

received her art education and illustration training at The Art Institute of Boston. In addition, she has a Master's Degree in Clinical Social Work and many years of experience as a psychotherapist. She lives in Eliot, Maine, with her family and three cats. In her leisure time she enjoys playing badminton with her 13 year old daughter, Rachel.

Ordering Information

For additional copies of this story book, send the title *(Cherubic Children's New Classic Story Book, Volume Two)* and $24.95 plus $5.00 shipping and handling (total $29.95) to:

Cherubic Press
P.O. Box 5306
Johnstown, PA, 15904-5036

BOOK ORDERS MAY BE MADE THROUGH OUR WEBSITE AT *www.gicsnet.com/cherubic*
with links through the Better Business Bureau of Western Pennsylvania, Pittsburgh, PA
e-mail us at *cherubic@gicsnet.com* or at *julieccht@aol.com*

Additional Titles available through Cherubic Press:

Cherubic Children's New Classic Story Book, Volume One. 1997 issue featured 31 healing and teaching stories in chapters on Adoption, Appreciating Others, Divorce, Family, Friends, Grief, Monsters & Ghosts, Nature, Self-Esteem, Special Kids, and Wisdom. $24.95 plus $5 shipping.

SOFT COVER CHILDREN'S PICTURE BOOKS

Grandpa's Berries, to help children understand Grief and Loss, Julie Dickerson, $11.95 + $2 ship.
The Broken Butterfly, to help children understand Responsibility and Forgiveness $11.95 + $2 ship.
Patrick Loves Peaches, to help children understand Loyalty and Peer Pressure (available Fall 1998)

God's Chosen Angel, a small angel's life in heaven, his birth on earth and then his return to heaven when he is called home. Touchingly written by Penny Tronzo after the loss of her 16 year old son, and whimsically illustrated by nationally syndicated cartoonist, Tom Gibb. $8.95 + $2 shipping.

Tia, the story of a Mouse and an Eagle by Angelo Peluso shows that even the smallest can overcome great odds with support and encouragement of loving parents. $8.95 + $2 shipping.

Angel Baby Gifts, a true American folk tale handed down from generation to generation in the author's family, now published for the first time. Written by Vickie Higgins and beautifully illustrated by Connie Spears, the story is set in the magical kingdom of Dreamland, and weaves a story full of love, hope and understanding. When your children ask why some babies are born with physical challenges, you will have this lovely story to share with them. $8.95 + $2 shipping.

Story Book of Native American Wisdom, by Donna J. Clovis and illustrated by Sally Lyn Platte. A dozen stories from the author's tribe of heritage gives an authentic and delightful glimpse of Native American storytelling as the author recollects the stories she grew up with. $9.98 + $2 shipping.

Poetry Patterns, by Karen A. Schuler, is a wonderful and unique guide to different types of poetry written in a light, entertaining style. Includes examples and explanations of couplet, triplet (tercet), quatrain, limerick, cinquain, lanterne, sestes, sepolet, haiku, tanka, free verse and concrete poetry, as well as how to write a poem. Excellent resource. $8.95 + $2 shipping, available Spring 1998.

Copyright Information

Li'l Pop Siggle	Denise I. Simmons	© 1996
We Can All Play	Nasreen Razack	© 1997
The Mouse House	Audrey Spilker	© 1996
A Special Story	Marion Kozlowski	© 1997
Helen Grace and her New Book	Maria Picciano	© 1997
Leaving the Nest	Janice Michael	© 1995
Sleepyland Slide	David Lasaine	© 1997
There's Always Tomorrow	Linda Bennington Valentino	© 1996
Grandma's Miracles	Diane-Ellen McCarron	© 1997
Dusty the Rag	Gina M. Pelletier	© 1997
Katie Finds a Friend	Beth Gallagher	© 1996
Allie and her New Friends	Nancy Boggs	© 1997
Squish the Fish and his Neighbors	Lynn A. Hayward	© 1996
Mulligan and Me	Theresa Williams	© 1997
The Monster Zapper	Diane Nelson	© 1997
Monsters No More	Susan Buffum	© 1996
The Deadest Fish	Mare Freed	© 1996
Freddy Fluff and Mrs. Benton's Birds	Gregory Brooks	© 1997
The Frog Croaked at Midnight	Pahl Rice	© 1997
Because I Am	Carla O'Brien	© 1997
The Balding Eagle	Herbert (Chip) Zyvoloski	© 1997
Rupert's Gift	John P. McCarthy	© 1997
The Perfect Shell	Juliet Shepherd	© 1997
Teddy Bears Can't Stand Up	Noah Margo	© 1997
My Brother Has a Brain Injury	Alvin Robert Cunningham	© 1997
Emily Said	Stacey Ann Taylor	© 1997
Where Does the Time Go	Scott Arney and Jennifer Arney	© 1997
The Cloud that Covered My Head	Ilana K. Levinsky	© 1997
Penelope and her Invisible Pooch	Carolyn Yencharis	© 1997
Jacob's Job	Diane Howell	© 1997
The People of Grey	Jan Fellerman	© 1997
Wind Spirit	Lois Kipnis and John P. DeCarlo	© 1997

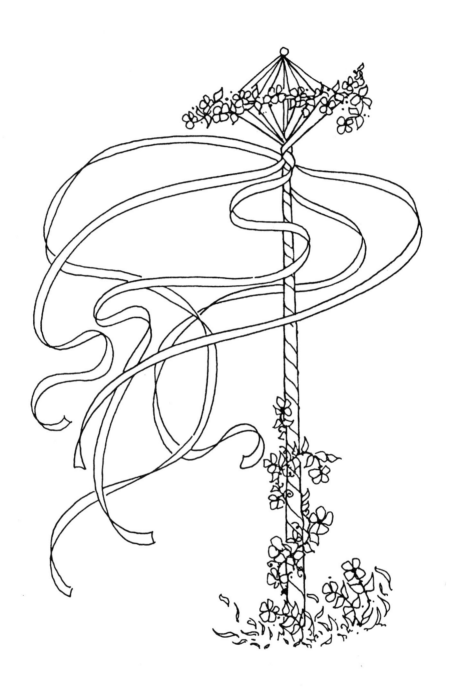